TO HAUNT A WITCH

The Jinx Hamilton Series - Book 8

JULIETTE HARPER

Chapter One

Don't ask me why I struck a match. Habit I guess. The first 30 years of my life, I didn't know I could snap my fingers and ignite a flame. Dragging a tiny blob of dried chemicals over a strip of sandpaper felt more natural.

Mistake number one.

Lucas and I stood in a dim, cluttered room in an abandoned house. The tall trees surrounding the structure blocked virtually all of the sun's rays. We needed more light. Other than that, I can't tell you *exactly* what I was thinking the moment the wick flared.

Mistake number two.

From the doorway behind me, Tori cried, "Jinksy! Don't do that!"

The warning came too late and surprised me so much, I stood there gaping at her until the burning match scorched my fingers. Swearing under my breath, I shook out the flame and resisted the urge to drop it. The whole place was a tinderbox waiting to ignite.

"Have you lost your mind?" I demanded.

"*Me?*" she said, outraged. "*You* just lit a hoodoo candle. What were you thinking?"

"That we needed some light in here."

Tori rolled her eyes. "Would you please stop being so literal? What were you *thinking?* What was your *intention* when you lit the candle?"

My intention?

"I don't know," I admitted. "I guess that I wanted to find this ghost so we can go home."

Mistake number three.

Let me hit rewind here and explain a few things. The afternoon I lit that candle, Tori, Lucas, Connor, Festus, Rube, and I had plans to set up "camp" in the deserted living room of a derelict house owned by the local Strigoi clan, the Ionescus. Those plans were about to change.

Four months earlier, we ventured into the In Between for a whole world-saving *thing* that garnered interesting results. For starters, we came back with reformed sorceress, Brenna Sinclair in tow and then there was the diplomatic firestorm I touched off.

I promised the Dark Druid we'd terminate the Agreement segregating the Middle Realm from the Otherworld and the Human Realm.

No, I did not consider the political consequences — something my grandfather, Barnaby Shevington, reminds me of daily during our mirror calls. I put him and a lot of other high-ranking Fae in the position of finishing what I started, and they're not happy with me—at all.

As the first flowers began to bloom that April, I did my best to keep my head down and stay out of the line of fire. Unfortunately, with Barnaby preparing to leave for England in less than two weeks to attend a summit conference of the Ruling Elders, I would be in charge of affairs in Shevington.

Every day he called me from the Valley to brief me on

some arcane administrative details. Secretly, I suspected he made the calls purely to have another excuse to grumble about my "impetuous action with little thought to the consequences for the delicate balance of the affairs of the realms."

I'd heard that line so many times it might as well have been tattooed on my forehead.

Honestly, I was more than a little annoyed myself. No one seemed to remember that at the time I made that promise to the Dark Druid, the Mother Tree's life was in danger and the state of North Carolina had been plunged into a modern Ice Age.

Hello, people? Priorities?

After what would go down in the record books as the Freak Freeze of '15, the residents of Briar Hollow struggled with the idea of "getting back to normal." The customers who drank coffee with us at the Witch's Brew tossed meteorological theories around thick and fast. The scenarios ranged from the End of Days to a coming apocalypse worthy of a *Walking Dead* script.

Tori and I nodded, made patient, non-committal sounds in the back of our throats, and kept our mouths shut. We knew exactly what happened on Monday, December 26, 2015, in the State of North Carolina. Creavit wizard Irenaeus Chesterfield, in league with Cailleach Bheur, the Queen of Winter, set in motion a plan to kill the Mother Oak.

Obviously, we couldn't discuss those events with our human patrons as they debated the merits of home generators and poured over survivalist websites on their tablets. We might not have known the true extent of the lingering fear the Freak Freeze generated, but we have the best free WiFi in town thanks to the fairy mound.

Over the past year, our shop has become an informal meeting space for a couple of book clubs and enthusiast groups like our chess players. Anything that keeps them in their chairs and drinking coffee is good for us. That means we know the current "hot" book in town, the fact that Dub Martin uses his knights aggressively, and how many MREs Jo Nell Sanders has stored up ahead of the next disaster.

The day Jo Nell made that announcement, I waited until she'd walked away from the counter to ask Tori, under my breath, "What's an MRE?"

"Meal ready to eat," she said. "Dub paid $1400 for a three-month supply from some outfit online. He told me he picked the package with chili mac and cheese, brownies, and coffee."

In the middle of Armageddon I guess worrying about cholesterol doesn't rank high on your list of concerns.

I'm ashamed to say that while our friends and neighbors tried to recover from the storm in the best way they knew how we enjoyed a break from magical chaos.

None of us believed Chesterfield was gone for good, but we had managed to thwart his biggest scheme yet. Wherever he was, the wizard was no doubt plotting his next move. In the meantime, we got on with our lives.

My parents were settled into their new sporting goods business at the end of the block past Chase's cobbler shop. These days Mom wears the Amulet of Caorunn, a gift from the Mother Rowan.

The artifact's specific power is to restore that which has faded. It's filled my mother with confidence and beguiling feistiness. She's taken over instructing Dad in the possibilities of his newly awakened magic, most of which he's channeling into enchanting fishing lures. Under the influence of my brother, Connor, the ultimate animal whisperer, our father is a new convert to the religion of "catch and release."

Dad has filled his shop with some of the most beautiful fly-fishing gear I've ever seen. The flies he ties and sells are already gaining a reputation for their ability to attract fish and slide effortlessly out of their mouths.

Tori's mom, Gemma, is in her element in the apothecary she's opened across the corner from George and Irma's grocery store. I would imagine human businesses of that type have to fool with all sorts of FDA regulations and permits, but magic cuts through that nonsense. Gemma packages her alchemical remedies as herbal lotions, potions, pills, and teas along with an array of blessings, crystals, charms, and yes candles.

We'll get back to the candles. I promise.

Brenna works with us part of the time, but more and more she wanders over to Gemma's. Without breaking down the complicated ancestry, Brenna is Gemma and Tori's living ancestor. We're going with the generic "aunt" for human purposes, but she's their many times great grandmother.

Considering we all believed Brenna was dead and thoroughly evil, the vibrant, vivacious woman who has come into our lives has been a pleasant surprise. I think it helps that she and DGI agent Greer MacVicar are contemporaries. Talking about places they've visited, people they've known and men they kept company with prevents either one of them from feeling out of time and place.

Until I saw Greer teeter on the edge of losing control during our time in the Middle Realm, I didn't appreciate how she walks a fine line every moment of her existence. As the baobhan sith, a Scottish vampire, she needs blood to survive. She always made managing that requirement sound easy. Now, I've stared into her emerald eyes gone black with hunger. "Easy" does not apply.

Technically, the local Strigoi clan, the Ionescus, are also vampires, but they don't drink blood. In their native state, they would drain the life energy of their human victims. Thanks to the intervention of science, however, the clan thrives on a steady diet of electricity. The generators they hauled down the mountain and installed at the local high school during the Freak Freeze saved the people of Briar Hollow.

Reclusive more by circumstance than choice, the Strigoi are suddenly local heroes, receiving invitations from their formerly suspicious neighbors, and showing up around town more often. Because of that, I wasn't surprised when Cezar Ionescu, the clan's leader, walked into the shop one sunny Monday morning.

I *was* surprised when he ordered a coconut cinnamon spice latte — and even more surprised that Tori knew how to stir up the disgusting concoction. I prefer coffee in my coffee.

"You're not going to drink that thing, are you?" I asked.

Cezar is a handsome man with angular, tanned features and jet-black hair going gray at the temples. He grinned at me over the rim of his cup.

"What did you expect me to drink?" he said. "Something with more protein?"

Vampire humor. They always go for the open vein.

"Very funny," I said. "You look more like a black coffee kind of guy."

"Blame my Romanian heritage for that. I confess I also have a weakness for sweet potato pie."

"Now *that*," I said, "is perfectly normal. But coconut and cinnamon? Cezar, that's flat *wrong*."

The Strigoi leader chuckled and took another sip of his drink, wiping away the frothy mustache it left behind.

"I am afraid, my friend, that my choice of libation is not the only wrong thing we must discuss. We have a problem."

No good ever comes of a reformed vampire announcing there's a problem at hand — especially when that hand is holding a coconut cinnamon latte.

Chapter Two

Since we had the store to ourselves, Cezar launched into a description of his "problem." For years, the Ionescus have quietly bought land abutting their property to build a buffer zone between themselves and their closest neighbors.

"The practice restricts potential temptation," he explained. "Although our appetites are well regulated, we cannot risk coming into contact with humans at inopportune moments. We also don't enjoy being put in a position to explain our extensive use of generators."

Without being asked, Tori handed Cezar a fresh coconut and cinnamon latte. "After the Freak Freeze, the whole town knows you guys have the best generators in the state."

"That's true," Cezar said, taking a deep whiff of his drink like he'd uncorked a $500 bottle of wine. "And thankfully the whole town feels indebted to us. The good people of Briar Hollow believe we are survivalists. Now, having been forced to endure a winter apocalypse themselves, they are less disposed to see us as unusual."

"So what's the problem?" I asked.

"Are you aware of the existence of an online paranormal program produced locally called *Haunted Briar Hollow?*"

I wanted to drop my head in my hands and groan. Not only was I "aware" of *Haunted Briar Hollow*, the damn series has become the bane of my existence.

Before Christmas, we briefly employed Mindy Mathis, who is, along with her friends, Nick and Kyle, one of the show's creators. We thought keeping an eye on the paranormal investigators by having one of them working in the store would be a good idea, but hiding our magical activities from a "civilian" proved too difficult.

Mindy quit before we could fire her when they secured funding for *Haunted Briar Hollow's* production. Since then, the trio has completed an episode on the courthouse haunt, the bumbling spirit of deceased Mayor Howard McAlpin.

With all the infrared camera work and ominous sound effects, the kids meant the footage to be scary. Instead, we laughed until we cried. Howie has problems with maintaining a full body apparition. On bad days, he's just a pair of walking spectral wingtips. The night of the *Haunted Briar Hollow* "ghost hunt," Howie managed a pretty decent manifestation — from the waist down.

Listening to Nick solemnly theorize the deeper meaning of the fifty percent apparition was one of the funniest things I've heard in years.

"Half in this world and half in another," Nick intoned, *"caught between the forces of life and death, the late Mayor's dedication to the people of Briar Hollow remains undiminished."*

In life, Howie applied dedication to one thing — lining his pockets.

If I'm going for the optimistic interpretation of things, *Haunted Briar Hollow* does support the stated mission of the local Town Square Business and Paranormal Association to get tourists interested in coming to our tiny burg during the "off seasons." We get lots of out-of-town business during the summer and fall, but the rest of the year, local revenues tend to dry up.

The Association's first fall festival proved to be such a success, plans are underway for the 2016 version, which Tori calls SpookCon2. Little does the committee know how much we contribute to the town's growing paranormal reputation.

Our friend Beau Longworth puts in several appearances a month as the local Civil War ghost. Additionally, he may or may not be dating local librarian and historical society president Linda Albert.

Because Beau still considers himself a married man, we don't tease him about the amount of time he spends with Linda painstakingly researching local history to buttress the paranormal claims. Beyond his covert, ghostly existence, Beau also has the inside track on all things supernatural in our neck of the woods. He's more or less the mayor of the local cemetery, which irks Howie no end.

Since the *Haunted Briar Hollow* kids showed up in town, we've all worked enough paranormal interest to be good for the local economy while hiding Briar Hollow's real connection to things not of this world.

"What have the *HBH* kids done now?" I asked Cezar, steeling myself for the answer.

"They've discovered an abandoned house on a piece of property we've owned since the 1930s," he replied. "We have known for some time that the place is haunted, undoubtedly by the spirit of the old man Anton allowed to live there. The house sits on a steep hillside, quite hard to reach, but it can sometimes be seen from the road through breaks in the trees. There have been reports of strange lights in the windows and around the building."

"Which, I'm guessing, the junior ghost hunters have taken upon themselves to investigate," I said.

"Exactly. We expelled them for trespassing, but I don't have a lot of confidence that they won't be back. After that ridiculous episode they produced about the late Mayor McAlpin, I suspect they're looking for a more complete haunting for their next production."

Tori snickered. "That episode about Howie is pure gold. I must have watched it a dozen times by now."

Cezar grinned. "It's rather popular at movie night in the compound as well."

The vampires do movie night? That ought to be an interesting playbill.

"How can we help, Cezar?" I asked.

"We were hoping that you could visit the property and persuade the ghost to relocate. Perhaps to the Briar Hollow Cemetery. I understand the local spectral community is quite active and welcoming."

That was an understatement. The first time I visited the place after dark, I thought I'd stepped onto the set of *Night at the Museum*. The memory made me smile. That was also the night I met Beau for the first time. Now, I couldn't imagine life without the stalwart colonel.

Before I could even answer Cezar and say yes, which I fully intended to do, Tori was off and running.

"Can we go up there for several days?" she asked enthusiastically.

"Of course," Cezar said. "Stay as long as you like."

Wait a minute? Several *days* to have a conversation with one ghost?

"Slow down, girl," I said. "I sense one of your bright ideas in the making, and I already don't think I like it."

That won me an "oh, please" expression before Tori launched into a description of an article she'd read online about the increasingly popular pastime of "champing" in the UK.

"It's camping in ancient abandoned churches," she enthused, turning to Cezar. "Does your old place have electricity and water?"

Looking more than a little amused, the Strigoi leader shook his head. "I can't promise much. The house has been abandoned for quite some time, but there is a well, which has been covered, so the water should be fresh."

Undaunted, Tori forged ahead. "No problem on the juice factor. We can go solar."

This conversation was getting away from me fast.

"We can go *solar?*" I said, staring at her like she'd lost her mind — which she tends to do from time to time. "We are *witches,* you know. I think we can manage to light a room or zap up a meal in a pinch."

"That," she said with conviction, "would be cheating. Get in the spirit of the adventure. We need to do something *different* for a change, Jinksy, and what's more different around here than acting like normal humans?"

Hard point to argue.

For his part, Cezar didn't seem eager to remain in the middle of our debate. "I assume you are willing to help us out with this issue?" he asked.

When I nodded, he went on, "Then take all the time you want to work out the details and the length of your stay. Call me when you're ready, and I'll give you directions. Obviously, we want to be discreet, and I would like this handled sooner rather than later."

I assured him we'd be in touch by the next day at the latest, which left me to deal with Victoria Andrews, Adventurer Extraordinaire all on my own — a task immediately derailed by the arrival of the afternoon regulars.

As I greeted the customers, I shot Tori a "we are not done" look, which she met with open-eyed and totally fake innocence.

After we closed the shop that evening, I dragged her into

the storeroom and demanded to know why she had a sudden urge to camp.

"It's not really like camping if you stay in a house," she insisted. "I'll bet this old place has tons of character. We need a break from all this magical intrigue. Let's go have some fun, and, well, I thought we could ask Connor to join us."

Now we were getting somewhere. Over the past few weeks, Tori and Connor had increasingly become an item, although they were still fairly quiet about their relationship.

When she went to Shevington, it was always on the pretext of getting some alchemical supplies or consulting with Moira, but Tori didn't get straw stuck in her hair running those errands.

My brother works in the Shevington stables.

Stables. Straw.

I didn't fall off the hay wagon yesterday.

Why my oldest friend was coy with me of all people about falling in love with my brother, I could not fathom, but I trusted she'd tell me more when she was ready.

"If you want to spend more time with my handsome brother, you don't need me in tow to do it, or a haunted house as a prop."

"No, but it would be fun." She paused, growing more serious and more nervous. "You're my best friend, Jinksy. I really like Connor. I want the three of us to be friends. You understand, right?"

In the long history of our friendship, this was the first time Tori ever sounded embarrassed talking to me about a guy. Clearly, things were getting more serious between her and Connor than I realized. She was asking for my approval, which was so sweet, I wanted to cry.

"I understand," I said, giving her an encouraging smile.

To my astonishment, she actually blushed. "Besides, all that," she went on in a rush of words, "Connor really hasn't had much of an opportunity to see the human realm. I know he'd jump at the chance to check out some cool old abandoned house."

If that was her story and she wanted to stick with it, I would play along. She was right, everything about our world fascinated my Shevington-raised older brother. Everyday items we take for granted he treats like wonders from an alien civilization.

Softening to the idea, I said, "It does sound like fun."

Understand that apart from my desire to support their relationship, this was a major concession on my part. I might have been a tomboy beating around the woods when I was a kid, but as an adult, bad room service is about as close to camping as I've ever wanted to get.

"You could bring Chase," she ventured warily, "or Lucas."

There it was. The conversation we'd been dancing around for weeks.

Okay. Fine. Months.

Give me a break. My love life has been complicated by lots of magical *stuff*. After our big adventure in the Middle Realm, I sort of got interested in Chase again, but as much as I love the guy in a "wow, he would be a great brother" kind of way, my werecat friend and protector can be downright stodgy.

Festus puts it more bluntly. "That kid of mine wouldn't know a good time if it walked up and smacked him in the whiskers."

That's not exactly true, but Chase does have a hit list of dependable but boring qualities. DGI Agent Lucas Grayson, on the other hand, is anything but boring. Handsome, rakish, adventuresome. The guy wears a fedora and a leather duster. He could *be* Indiana Jones.

"Probably . . . Lucas," I admitted haltingly.

Tori's eyes lit up. "Oh. My. *God*. You finally decided to pick one of them?"

"Slow down. I didn't say I'd picked anyone."

"But you have, haven't you," Tori said, nailing me with her "don't lie to me" face.

She was between me and the door of the storeroom, so there was nowhere to run. Nodding weakly, I said, "Yeah, kinda. But what am I going to say to Chase?"

"You're going to tell him the truth. Seriously, Jinksy, it's way past time you put these guys out of their misery."

"Okay," I said uncertainly, "but I have to talk to Chase before we say anything to Connor and Lucas. I don't want to spring this on him."

"Then get to talking. Chase is downstairs in the lair, and you told Cezar we'd call him in the morning. No time like the present."

What can I say? When no one is around to do it for me, I'm perfectly capable of throwing myself right under the nearest bus.

Chapter Three

W hen we went down to the lair, I caught a minor break. Chase wasn't there. Even with Tori pretty much forcing me to do the right thing, I didn't relish the idea of asking the man to step into my private alcove in front of everyone.

Beau, Brenna, and Myrtle are in residence full-time, but it's not unusual to find 10 to 12 people — usually waiting to be fed — down in the lair at the end of the day. Which leaves our Brownie friend, Darby, in a state of ecstatic hospitality. The little guy loves laying out a spread on the big conference table, and I have to admit those huge family dinners are the highlight of my day as well.

Lately, the fairy mound has taken to reinventing itself according to our needs. During the Freak Freeze it went into emergency shelter mode, materializing bedrooms and even an indoor relief station for my father's dogs.

The mound connects all of our shops. As soon as Mom and Dad moved into their building, they instantly found an entrance to the fairy mound in the basement waiting for them.

I knew that if Chase wasn't in the lair, he was probably at

his shop. Earlier in the month he received an order from a wealthy equestrian to make three pairs of riding boots. The project had been his passion since, and the delivery deadline was looming.

All I had to do was negotiate a short passageway, and I would be in the cobbler shop where we could have our conversation in private. Anyone surprised I stalled for time?

In my defense, the scene Tori and I stumbled upon made that beyond easy, courtesy of one werecat and three irate raccoons.

Rube and his "associates" Leon and Marty sat around a low table in front of the hearth playing poker with Festus. As Tori and I came down the stairs, Rube slapped his paw on the table, sending chips flying in all directions.

"McGregor, you stinking werecat scum, you're marking the cards with your claws."

Festus regarded his black-masked, striped opponent with an impassive expression. "Stinking? I'm not the one who spends the bulk of my time ratting around in sewers."

At that, Marty bared his teeth, and Leon growled, "Who you calling a rat?"

Before I could say anything, Greer looked over the top of her book. Arguably, she's the most dangerous member of the team, but she spends a remarkable amount of time quietly reading in her favorite wingback chair.

All she said was, "Gentlemen," but the warning glow in her green eyes spoke volumes.

Rube lowered his voice, but he didn't back down. "Give a coon a break, Red! He's cheating. You look at those cards. They got claw holes up in the corners."

Time for me to get into the conversation. I cleared my throat, and four furry heads swiveled in my direction.

A flicker of wary caution came into the werecat's countenance before he said smoothly, "Well, good evening, Jinx. My heavens you are looking lovely."

Uh, right. That's all it took to tell me the old rascal was guilty as sin.

"Give me that deck of cards."

Rube reached over and grabbed the cards out of Festus' paws, using his own clever black hands to gather up the rest of the deck from his pals. When he handed me the complete set, I fanned the cards out and held them up to the light.

Sure enough, there were tiny holes in the upper right-hand corner of exactly 16 cards — Festus had marked all the face cards and aces, with the latter sporting two holes instead of one.

"Festus," I scolded, "I am ashamed of you. Cheating at cards."

"Cheat," he said, "is a strong word. I was merely strengthening my advantage."

Mumbling an incantation under my breath, I ran my hand over the deck before giving it back to Rube. "The holes are gone, and I put a protection spell on the pasteboard. He can't mark them again."

"Much appreciated, Jinx," the raccoon said, baring his sharp teeth in a broad grin. "You're an okay dame, but you need to talk to him about dealing off the bottom of the deck, too."

At that, Greer slammed her book shut. "Give me those cards, and someone pour me a glass of Scotch. I'm dealing now."

Her words put a droop in Festus' ears but settled the matter of any more nefarious play. That wouldn't be happening with the baobhan sith on the case.

Then, to make matters worse for the werecat, my mother walked into the lair — in time to pick up on the gist of the conversation and add a lecture of her own to my rebuke.

"Festus James McGregor, you should be ashamed of yourself!"

Even though I wasn't the one in trouble, I cringed. I can't tell you how many times I have heard those same words prefaced by my full Southern name — Norma Jean Hamilton.

I don't know why, but when mothers pull out the three-name weapon the threat level pops the lid off the DEFCON meter.

Beside me, I saw Tori flinch as well. She's Victoria Tallulah Andrews. More syllables for menacing emphasis, and trust me, her mom can hit every note.

You wouldn't think a ginger tomcat could blanch, but I swear to you Festus' fur paled. He's seriously in love with my mother and never wants to be on her bad side.

"I was just having fun with them, Kelly," he said contritely.

"Give them their money back this instant."

Festus didn't like it, but he did as he was told. The game started over under Greer's watchful supervision. Tori went over to her alchemical worktable. She and her mother were deep in the middle of a research project on candle magic in the name of retail profit.

Gemma already had candles for sale at the apothecary and Tori was considering adding similar items to our inventory. Their challenge was to come up with items carrying sufficient enchantment to provide real benefit without unwanted magical consequences.

To be more appealing to tourists, they were keeping their creations in line with the regional hoodoo tradition — not to be confused with voodoo.

Voodoo is an actual religion, while hoodoo is a system of folk magic blending pagan traditions with ancient practices and European religion.

Hoodoo practitioners draw on their individual power intermingled with minerals, herbs, personal possessions, and even animal parts to work their magic. I didn't find out until recently that many women in our magical line have posed as hoodoo witches to be more free to use their powers in the human realm.

Tori's Granny Mo taught her about herbal potions and instructed her in superstitions long before we learned the truth about our heritage. Thankfully that early exposure allowed Tori to believe me when I inherited what I believed to be a haunted store.

Gemma paired that folk knowledge with her study of alchemy to develop the items she sold in the apothecary. Since the people of Briar Hollow had regarded my Aunt Fiona as a "witch woman" when she owned the store, they hadn't blinked an eye over Gemma's wares — and the tourists were eating it up.

While Tori set to work, I went over and joined my mother who was still casting suspicious looks at Festus.

"That three name thing is deadly," I observed.

"It always worked with you." Then, lowering her voice, she said, "Thank heavens Festus doesn't know I can never stay mad at him."

Out of the corner of my eye, I saw the old cat look up suddenly. He heard what Mom said, which is exactly what she intended. She might fuss at the werecat for his often outrageous behavior, but she'd never do anything to hurt him. The two of them have an inseparable bond that has only grown stronger over the last year.

In the beginning, when Mom's long suppressed powers came back online, I think Dad was a little jealous of Festus, but they got that worked out. Mom doesn't have eyes for anyone but my father, but she and Festus have been through a lot together.

"Are you here for your session with Myrtle?" I asked.

Given the recent developments with the Mother Rowan,

the aos si, suggested my mother resume her formal magical studies. The exact content of the lessons remains a secret, but instinct tells me they're delving into far more esoteric subjects than spells and potions.

Mom nodded. "We're taking the portal to Roslin."

"How long will you be gone?"

"A couple of hours. The Mother Rowan talks in the same kind of riddles the Oak uses. The longer the conversation with her the more I think my head is going to explode."

"Has she told you more about why you were given the Amulet of Caorunn?"

In response, I received nothing but a cryptic smile.

"Okay, fine," I said with annoyance, "don't tell me."

"I can't, honey," Mom said. "The trees haven't given us permission yet."

When my mother received the Amulet, she immediately announced, "The Oak and the Rowan have become one." — And not a *one* of us has a clue what the heck that means.

"Where's Dad?"

"He went out to the river. He wanted to get in some casting practice. He and the dogs will be along later. What are you doing tonight?"

Everyone around us seemed occupied. Beau was at the rolltop desk working with Glory, his spectral coonhound, Duke, glowing faintly at his feet.

Together, Beau and Glory have assumed responsibility for an enormous undertaking. The fairy mound is a major Fae archive, but one with an incomplete catalog system. Tori wrote an app to make it easier to locate artifacts in the collection, but a shocking number of items still sit on the shelves without locator numbers.

Before Irenaeus Chesterfield cursed Glory to live her life as a miniature green witch, the woman worked as an archivist for the state of North Carolina. Getting our collection in proper order has become her passion. She spends hours cruising the stacks on her broom snapping pictures with her smartphone and taking notes on her iPad.

We've become skilled at shrinking everyday items for her use. She lives in a dollhouse replica of Graceland, which would be one of North Carolina's most luxurious pieces of real estate had it been full size.

Rodney, sat on Beau's shoulder. He caught my eye and raised a paw in greeting. I blew him a kiss, which he caught and pressed to his heart.

"Let's go in the alcove," I said. "I need to check on the cats."

After my father's dogs became regulars in the lair, it didn't seem right to leave my cats — Zeke, Yule, Xavier, and Winston — alone in my apartment. Myrtle worked out a boundary spell to prevent cross-species clashes and to keep the guys from wandering into the archive and getting lost. For the most part, however, they stay flaked out in my alcove, which includes a recessed space with a cozy bed.

They have their own feline-sized staircase that opens into my living room two levels above. There is nothing cats like better than being able to come and go at will, and they enjoy spending time with Festus. The werecat speaks flawless Felinese, and has, alas, ignited a higher level of attitude in my furry friends, which isn't something I would have thought possible.

Mom followed me without comment but arched an eyebrow when I drew the sound-blocking curtain closed.

"Honey, is everything okay?" she asked with concern.

After I relayed the details of our conversation with Cezar and the highlights of Tori's camping plan, I hesitated.

"You want to take someone with you, too," Mom said gently. "And that someone isn't Chase."

Nodding miserably, I said, "Tori says I have to talk to him about it tonight."

"Tori is right."

"How do I do that?"

Mom leaned forward in her chair and rested her hands over mine. "You just do it, Norma Jean. Chase deserves honesty from you. The two of you didn't make it as a couple, but he's your sworn protector. You have to work together. I know what I'm talking about here."

That opened the door for me to ask a question I'd wondered about for months. "Did you know that Festus was in love with you back then?"

"Always, and if I hadn't met your father, I could have loved him in return. Festus may talk tough, but he's one of the gentlest souls you could hope to find in this realm or any other. My choice hurt him, but it didn't destroy our affection for one another. Festus is *my* sworn protector. It's a special connection, Jinx. You don't want to lose Chase as a friend. Talk to him."

Chapter Four

Kelly and Myrtle sat together in Rosslyn Chapel outside Edinburgh, Scotland waiting for Katrina Warner. Kelly glanced at her watch and silently worked the time conversion — a quarter of ten at night. If everything went well, they'd be back home in time to join the others for supper in Briar Hollow thanks to the five-hour time difference.

Turning to Myrtle, she said, for the third time, "Are you sure we're supposed to be in here?"

The aos si smiled. "I was 'in here' when this chapel was being built in the 15th century. I hardly intend to seek anyone's permission to visit now."

"That's not exactly something you can tell a security guard," Kelly pointed out.

"I have cloaked our presence. Even if a guard were to walk through, he would see nothing but empty pews. We are free to enjoy in peace what William Sinclair wrought on this ground."

Kelly studied the arcade of exquisitely carved pillars supporting the structure. "When will we bring the girls here?"

"When the Mother Trees tells us the time has come,"

Myrtle replied. "What lies ahead for Jinx and Tori must be a journey of discovery that takes them, at last, to Oak Island. We can't interfere with the course of those events."

Kelly sighed. "I think I liked it better when I didn't know about any of this."

"No, you didn't. Before you were given the Amulet of Caorunn, you lived with deep dread over what might lay ahead for your daughter. Now, you are merely eager for the great changes to commence."

"I'd like to tell you that you're wrong," Kelly sighed, "but you're not. We have so much to accomplish in the coming months. I am ready for it all to begin."

A voice behind her said, "As am I, but as usual, the Mother Rowan is taking her bloody time, and I can't say the Oak is much better."

A trim blonde draped in a warm tartan cloak sank into the pew beside Kelly. "*Ciamar a tha thu?*" she asked in Gaelic.

"Good," Kelly answered, "and you?"

"Other than the fact that my great lout of a business partner is probably stinking drunk at the pub again," Katrina laughed, "I'm good as well."

Myrtle clicked her tongue. "Findlay did not learn his lesson when the Amulet was taken from him?"

"He did not. If anything, I think it drove him to hold tighter to the bottle."

The trio fell silent for a few minutes, absorbing the energy of the chapel and its complex imagery. Finally, Myrtle said, "Before we go to speak with the Mother Rowan, tell me, is there talk among the Women of the Craobhan about the impending negotiations?"

"Only that Jinx made a bold and perhaps reckless move in making such a promise to Fer Dorich," Katrina said, adding hastily to Kelly, "meaning no offense to your daughter."

"None taken," Kelly assured her. "Jinx did make a bold

move with the Dark Druid, but the coming events were set in motion long before the kidnapping of the Queen of Summer."

"True," Katrina agreed. "There is one bit of gossip I can share. The witches in London say Elder Isherwood is not one bit happy."

"Good," Myrtle said, rising from her seat. "The thought of Reynold Isherwood resting poorly on his pillow pleases me no end. Now come, we cannot keep the Great Tree waiting."

WHEN I OPENED the door to the cobbler shop, I heard blue-grass music coming from the front. "Chase," I called out, "do you have a minute?"

The music switched off mid-tune.

"Sure. Come on in."

I found Chase at his workbench wearing his long, leather apron. "Hi," I said, "how's the project coming?"

"Good. What do you think?"

He leaned back revealing a gleaming pair of tall ebony boots he'd been polishing.

"Wow, they're beautiful."

The admiration was sincere. Chase is a meticulous craftsman.

"Thank you. The client didn't put any limitation on the cost. Touch the leather. It's a once-in-a-lifetime experience."

As directed, I trailed my fingers over the buttery soft material, careful not to leave fingerprints behind.

"Oh!" I breathed. "You're right. That is sinful. I don't guess you have enough left over to make a handbag?"

"I might," Chase grinned. "So to what do I owe the honor of this visit? Not that I'm complaining you understand." He moved forward to give me a kiss, which I deflected into a hug before pulling out the second stool and sitting down.

"Cezar Ionescu paid us a visit today," I said.

Accurately sensing the tension in my mood, Chase asked, "Is that a good thing or a bad thing?"

Since I'd just told the same story to my mother, I had a synopsis of the conversation with the Strigoi in my mind. Chase listened with an inscrutable expression.

When I got to the part about Tori's idea to turn the whole thing into a camping trip and her desire to ask Connor along, I began to stumble over my words. The longer I talked, the more heat rose to my face until Chase finally stepped in.

"You came here to tell me you don't want me to come along," he said quietly, "which means you are probably planning to ask Lucas to join you."

I opened and shut my mouth like a fish out of water. First my mother and now him? Was I the last person to figure out which man I was supposed to be dating? I nodded dumbly.

"Okay," he said, "my turn to talk. I like the way we've been getting along for the last few months. I don't want that to change, but let's be honest, Jinx, the spark we felt back in the beginning isn't there anymore, is it?"

An unexpected wave of sadness washed over me. "No, it isn't."

"It's okay," he said. "People change. You've embraced your magical heritage and made it your own. At the end of the day, I'm happy sitting here in my shop making boots. A whole new world has been laid out in front of you. You want to explore it. Lucas is a good explorer. Actually, he's a good guy, too."

"That's not how you felt when he first showed up. I know you're on friendly terms now, but that's only because of what happened in the Middle Realm. Why the bad blood between you two before that?"

Chase scrubbed at his face tiredly. "How much has Dad told you?"

"Only that you and Lucas were friends when you were

boys. Festus says he doesn't know what caused the animosity either."

Surprise registered on his features. "Really? I would have thought he and Morris talked about it."

"Who is Morris?"

"Morris Grayson. Lucas is his nephew. Morris is the head of the DGI."

It was my turn to be surprised. "That's a detail Lucas left out. I did meet his Uncle Owain though."

"Owain is an uncle on his mother's side," Chase explained. "Morris is a paternal uncle. He and Dad have been acquainted for years."

"Okay, all of that is interesting, but none of it tells me what happened between you and Lucas."

Chase looked down, his tanned face flushing slightly. Understanding suddenly dawned on me. I don't know why it never occurred to me before.

"Who was she?" I asked, reminding myself that I did not have the luxury of feeling jealous right in the middle of breaking up with a man — again.

"A girl we grew up with," Chase said. "A girl I loved very much who had eyes only for Lucas . . . like you do."

You know how people say they wish the floor would open up and swallow them? That would have been a complete blessing.

"Chase," I said, my voice thick with emotion as I caught hold of his hands, "that's not true. I do love you. I will always love you, but it would never work for us to be together. You won't ever stop trying to tell me what to do in the interest of taking care of me or making decisions you think are for my own good without talking to me first. We can deal with that as friends, but not as partners."

He looked up, letting me see the misery he felt. "If I hadn't broken up with you over that business with Malcolm Ferguson, we would have been fine."

"Maybe," I conceded, "but sooner or later something would have come along that would have had the same effect. You can't help it, Chase. You were raised to protect the Daughters of Knasgowa. No matter how much you may love me, to some degree you're always going to see taking care of me as your job."

When he started to protest, I held up my hand to stop him. "Don't. At first, that hurt me a lot, but I understand now. Of course, there's always going to be a part of me that wonders what might have been, but if we can have the kind of friendship Festus and my mother have, I'll consider myself a blessed woman. Can we do that?"

His hands tightened on mine. "We can," he said, his voice cracking.

I stood up, moved into his arms, and kissed him — a real kiss, not the kind of pity kiss you throw a guy on your way out the door. Chase deserved better than that from me.

When our lips parted, Chase leaned his forehead against mine and whispered, "If Lucas Grayson hurts you, I'll make him wish he was never born."

It wasn't until hours later that I realized I hadn't asked him what happened to that girl.

CHASE and I walked back to the lair together. He didn't want to come at first, but if he'd missed supper, everyone would have wanted to know why. This family I've put together is a perceptive bunch though. Neither one of us said a word, but everyone seemed to realize instantly that we'd had "the" difficult conversation.

"Boy," Festus ordered, "come sit by your old man before one of these coons stinks up my dinner plate."

Since Rube, Marty, and Leon were fastidiously washing their hands at the time the remark won Festus a round of pointed looks. In response, he disdainfully licked first his right and then his left front paw.

"Satisfied?" he demanded of the assemblage.

Rube hopped up on the chair nearest Greer and said, "You wouldn't catch me eating with my paws in that condition. Case of botched lizard waiting to happen if you ask me."

"I'll botch you," Festus hissed in response. As the banter flew back and forth at a fast and furious pace, Chase and I smiled at each other across the table. Sometimes the best kind of comfort isn't delivered with soft words and commiserating expressions.

Amity Prescott plopped a liberal helping of mashed potatoes on her plate before passing the bowl to Beau and putting me in the crosshairs of her acerbic tongue.

"Jinx, you have been avoiding me."

Since that's exactly what I'd been doing, I didn't bother to deny the accusation.

"We have to narrow down the list of coven prospects and get started on the second round of interviews," she continued. "Don't make me take this up with your grandfather."

Great. As if Barnaby wasn't put out with me enough already over my promise to the Dark Druid.

"Do we have to do that tonight?" I asked, hiding my misery in a triple helping of fried okra.

"Yes, we do. I told you we have to have at least half a coven in place before Halloween this year."

From the staircase, Gemma said, "Half a coven would be 6.5 witches, Amity. Who are you planning on cutting in half?"

Behind her, Brenna put her hand over her mouth to stifle a

laugh. The two women joined us at the table with Amity looking daggers through Gemma.

"Very funny You know perfectly well we need seven witches at minimum and we only have five at the moment. We can continue to use Fiona as the sixth for the time being, but she's adamant about retiring."

That's when inspiration struck. Counting me and Tori, our mothers, and Amity, we did have five, but there was a sixth incredibly powerful witch sitting right across the table from me that no one had even considered.

"Fine," I said, "then I've made my choice. Brenna. That gives us seven for the time being."

Everyone froze with their silverware in mid-air.

"Is there a problem?" I asked, throwing down the rhetorical question like a gauntlet. "She's probably the most powerful witch in the room, and she's on our side now. Why shouldn't she be in the coven?"

Brenna looked at me with real affection in her lovely eyes. I swear she and Greer were both produced at the same factory. Either that or drop-dead gorgeous redheads with green eyes are standard stock in Scotland.

"Jinx," she said softly, "you do me a great honor, one that no fellow witch has ever extended, but I don't know how such a choice would go over in the Fae world. Perhaps you should choose another."

That did nothing but make me more determined. "I'm the Witch of the Oak. The choice is mine and mine alone to make. If you want this, you're in."

Still uncertain, Brenna looked over at Gemma and Tori. "What do the two of you say?"

"I say it's about damned time," Tori replied, spearing a piece of fried chicken. "This is a family business after all."

"My sentiments exactly," Gemma said. "Amity, that would be three votes in Brenna's favor."

From the stacks near Myrtle's quarters, my Mother spoke up. "Five. My vote, and I have Fiona's proxy."

Turning my attention back to Amity, I simply said, "Majority rules. Brenna's in the coven. Questions?"

Although her face was almost purple, the older witch nodded curtly. "Very well," she barked, but under her breath, I thought I heard her mutter something like "Creavit trash."

Maybe I was in a mood to pull rank, or maybe I was fed up with Amity's increasingly sour disposition. Regardless, I don't like to see people denied second chances they've earned the hard way.

Brenna broke her deal with the darkness to become Creavit by passing through fire — literally. I've seen the scars from the burns and heard the pain of the memory.

Once the Freak Freeze ended, Brenna sat down with Tori, the moms and me and invited us to ask her anything. Two bottles of wine later, we better understood the things that drove her to become Creavit and the price she paid for her decision.

The woman had not led an easy life. I respected her for coming back from her bad choices, owning her misdeeds, and earnestly working to make amends.

"If you have something to say, Amity, have the courage and the integrity to say it aloud," I snapped.

This time the silence that fell over the room seemed to suck all the air out of the space. Amity had gotten far too used to talking to me like I was still the clueless young woman who inherited the store from my aunt. That needed to stop.

Our eyes locked and, after several seconds, Amity blinked.

"My apologies, Witch of the Oak," she said formally. "I would not presume to question your choices."

Yeah, right, but at least I'd made her back down in front of everyone.

"Good," I said. "Now that we have that settled, could somebody please pass me the cornbread?"

Chapter Five

L ucas didn't show up for dinner. Before Greer went back to dealing cards for Festus and the raccoons, I beckoned her off to one side and asked after her partner's whereabouts.

"The laddie had an errand in Patagonia. He'll be along tomorrow."

Treading carefully, I asked, "Could you get a message to him tonight?"

The baobhan sith eyed me appraisingly. "I could, so long as the message is in his best interests."

Greer made no secret about her disapproval of the indecision with which I'd approached the question of which man would be in my life. At Christmas time she threatened me, albeit in a pleasant way, if I did anything to hurt Lucas.

Thankfully, he came to me after the Freak Freeze and suggested we remain friends until I knew who and what I wanted. Erring on the side of caution, I asked him to be sure and convey that information to Greer. I had no desire to find myself in the position of dealing with an angry Scottish vampire in mother hen mode.

Lucas did as I asked, and Greer lightened up, but my question had her radar pinging at full strength.

Lowering my voice, I said, "I had a talk with Chase. Cezar Ionescu asked us to relocate a ghost haunting one of his mountain properties. Tori wants to turn the whole thing into a camping trip. I plan to ask Lucas to come with me."

"Lucas and not Chase."

"Correct."

She nodded approvingly. "Do you want me to tell Lucas about the camping trip?"

"No. I want you to tell him that I'd like him to have dinner with me tomorrow night away from the lair."

That won me a smile. "A message I will gladly convey and one he will happily receive. What time?"

"About six if he can make it. We'll leave from here."

"The laddie will be here," Greer said, "if he has to elbow his way through every portal between Patagonia and Briar Hollow."

I started to ask why he was in Patagonia, but I wouldn't get any more of an answer than I received when he was in Istanbul or Khartoum or Bora Bora. There were many reasons I wanted to be with Lucas, but honestly? I was hoping he'd finally tell me what they heck he does on his "errands."

After my conversation with Greer, I had to arrange the major component of my plan. Location. Location. Location. If that part didn't work out, I wasn't sure how I was going to orchestrate the dinner.

Before I inherited the store, Tori and I both worked at Tom's Diner in our hometown, Cotterville. Every spring, Tom closes up shop for a week to hide in the woods with a stack of books and his fishing pole.

If he'd let me, I wanted to commandeer the diner for a night. Tori was so adamant about not using magic on our impending trip into the mountains; I thought it would be fun to present the idea to Lucas in the place that was my world before I even knew real magic existed.

Well, that, and we would have some privacy in the back dining room.

I went into my alcove, drew the curtain, and took out my cell phone. Another perk of living over a fairy mound; excellent reception without the minutes ever hitting our billing plans.

Tom answered with his usual gruff greeting. "What? I don't have all day."

"Good to talk to you, too," I said dryly. "I can see your manners haven't improved since we've been gone."

"Jinx? Your store flopped yet? If you've called to beg for a job, don't bother. I don't put ingrates to work."

All that line of bilge succeeded in doing was confirming the old coot missed me.

"You wish," I shot back. "Is this your week to go on vacation?"

"It is."

"I'd like to ask a favor."

A snort came across the line. "I knew you were after something. What do I get out of the deal?"

"You haven't even heard what I want yet."

"I don't go into a negotiation unless I can see all the chips on the table."

Leaving out the complicated details, I told him I wanted to use the back room the next night to have dinner with someone special. In exchange, Tori and I would supply fresh pies for the diner for a month.

"Since when did you two take up baking?" he asked suspiciously.

"Since we put in the espresso bar," I said, which was only a slight lie. Tom didn't need to know Darby would be the one baking the pies.

"Fruit or custard?"

"Both," I said, knowing that's what it would take to seal the deal.

This time the derisive snort was louder and thoroughly triumphant. "Ha! You best not take up haggling for a living. You roll over too easy. Okay, the place is yours. You still got your keys?"

When Tori and I quit, we both tried to give our keys back, but Tom wouldn't take them, declaring, "Somebody has to be able to get in here to keep my abandoned carcass from stinking up the place when I die a lonely, forgotten old man."

Did I mention Tom has a flair for the melodramatic?

"I still have my keys. Has the alarm code changed?"

"Lord. Why would I do that? I can barely remember the numbers now. The alarm company charged me for three emergency calls last month for setting the damned thing off by accident."

Just three? That was a good month.

"Tom, the numbers are your birthday."

"Exactly. Who the hell wants to remember something like that?"

We batted back a few more good-natured insults, and Tom exacted an unnecessary promise that I would leave the place as clean as I found it, lock up, and set the alarm.

Now, as for the meal itself, I confess I planned to *kind of* cheat by asking Darby to fix a basket of food for us.

You sticklers for detail can hush.

I did Lucas a favor. I have many talents. Cooking isn't among them. With Darby in charge, there would be plenty of food and all at the right temperature when we were ready to eat.

Don't judge me until you try out life with a house brownie. There is no — as in *zero* — chance of going back.

Before I could call Darby to discuss meal planning, the

curtain over the alcove door flared and Rodney scampered up the arm of my chair.

"Well, hello there," I said, holding my hand out to the handsome black and white rat. "Why aren't you watching a movie with Glory in Graceland East?"

Rodney held out one paw and made a zooming motion.

"She's off on her broom, eh? I don't know how she manages to navigate the stacks without getting lost. She and Beau are making incredible progress with the catalog.

The rat nodded, then turned solemn eyes toward me, circled his paw over his heart, and then mimed breaking something in two.

"No. I don't have a broken heart. How did you know Chase and I talked?"

Dropping his head, Rodney acted out someone eating slowly and quietly.

"Yeah, he didn't have much to say at dinner, did he? Chase is going to need some time to get used to this."

Looking at me with questioning eyes, Rodney put on an invisible hat.

"Yes," I grinned, "I picked Lucas. I'm going to tell him tomorrow night."

When he held up his tiny paw in approval of the announcement, I used my index finger to give Rodney one-fifth of a high five

"Cezar Ionescu came into the shop today and asked us to go up in the mountains to check out a haunted property he owns," I explained. "Tori wants to make a camping trip out of it and ask Connor, so I'm going to ask Lucas."

Rodney's eyes took on a triumphant gleam. He pointed to his chest.

"No," I started to reply on reflex, "you can't . . ."

The rat stopped me with a classic "talk to the paw" move.

"Oh, crap," I said, deflating instantly. "I promised you that you could go on the next adventure, didn't I?"

Rodney nodded so vigorously his whiskers bounced up and down.

"Okay, fine, you can go, but keep this to yourself until I get everything set up with Lucas. Deal?"

The rat gave me a thumbs-up before running up my arm and snuggling under the collar of my shirt. That's one of the reasons Rodney gets away with so much around here. He may be little, but he completely understands the power of a good hug.

GLORY FLEW CAUTIOUSLY down the narrow passageway. She knew it led to the cobbler shop, but she'd never been here before and didn't want to risk smacking into anything. It wouldn't do for the others to find her knocked out cold. Then she'd have to explain why she'd decided to seek out Chase McGregor and if Festus heard, there'd be no end to the teasing.

Up ahead, a thin sliver of light told her she'd reached her destination. She contemplated the crack between the closed door to the shop and the frame. Too small for her to fly through without working her only magical ability.

Concentrating hard on the way her body felt, Glory exhaled mightily, pleased to feel her form compress. After six good outbursts of air, she was as thin as a piece of paper. Sliding easily through the crack, the little witch reversed the process plumping herself back to normal.

She smoothed her hair nervously and ran a hand down the black pantsuit Greer helped her pick out. With newly scaled down Louboutins on her feet and tiny diamond earrings from Cartier, Glory felt elegant for the first time in her life. Who knew that all she'd ever needed was to lose some weight and get a vampire for a life coach?

Following the strains of an old bluegrass ballad emanating from the front of the shop, Glory flew silently through the building. Chase sat at his workbench cutting leather for a second pair of riding boots.

When the song ended, Glory used the front of her broom to tap on the doorframe. "Hi Chase. Can I come in?"

Turning toward the door, Chase smiled when he saw her — a smile so beautiful she thought her heart might stop in her chest. "Hi, Glory," he said, turning off the CD player. "You haven't been here before, have you?"

As she floated slowly across the room, Glory said, "I haven't. I hope you don't mind me just inviting myself like this."

"Of course not," he said, clearing a space for her on the table. "I'm glad to see you. What's up?"

Glory touched down on the workbench and stepped off her broom, trying as hard as she could to look taller than her 11.5 inches.

"I wanted to see if you were okay. You didn't say much at dinner. Rodney and I talked about it, and we think maybe you and Jinx broke up for good."

Chase shook his head. "So much for hiding it from everyone in the interest of avoiding drama. We did break up, and yes, I'm okay. A little sad, but okay. How are you?"

The question made her eyes go wide with surprise. "Me?"

"Yes, you're upset that they haven't asked you to join the coven, aren't you?"

"Oh," she breathed in an awestruck voice, "how did you know?"

"I was watching you when they were talking about Brenna becoming a member. I'm sorry if they hurt your feelings."

Glory set her mouth in a stubborn line. "They didn't hurt

my feelings, they made me mad! I mean, for heaven's sake! I look more like a witch than any of them do."

Struggling to keep a straight face, Chase said, "I'm afraid the job takes more than looks. Other than being able to ride your broom and make yourself flat, do you have other powers?"

The tiny witch wilted. "No, but only because no one will take the time to teach me."

"That's actually a fair point. You should talk to Jinx about that."

"It is? I should?"

This time Chase did laugh. "Yes, and yes. Why don't I make us some tea? You can keep me company while I work. Do you like old mountain music?"

Glory's face lit up. "I just adore the Carter Family. That reunion album that came out in 1997? The one from when Mother Maybelle and Sara got back together to sing in 1966? That's my favorite."

"Then you're in luck," Chase said, flipping through his CDs, "because I have it. You know, I met Mother Maybelle one time backstage at the Opry."

"You were *backstage* at the *Opry*?" Glory gasped. "Oh, Chase, you have to tell me *everything*!"

As he began the story, Glory thought to herself that Jinx Hamilton must be the biggest fool in the state of North Carolina to give up a man as handsome and kind as Chase McGregor.

If only someone could find a way to make her normal sized again, and if by some miracle he would notice her, Glory believed she might be happier than she would ever have imagined possible in the whole world.

Even happier than she would have been if she'd ever been blessed enough to meet Elvis himself, and that was saying something!

Chapter Six

The next morning, Tuesday, I called Cezar and told him we were good to go, but that we couldn't leave for at least a couple of days. I had awakened to an email from Tori with a new bright idea — one that I liked — give the Haunted Briar Hollow kids something to keep them busy while we worked on rehoming the problem ghost.

When I went downstairs, Tori had our coffee ready as usual. Instead of going over the latest supply order or tending to the kind of business that filled our working breakfasts, we hatched a counterintelligence operation.

Cue the music for Agent Double O'Darby, Brownie of Mystery.

Here's what we cooked up.

The HBH kids rent the old Fish Pike house. Fish was a crazy werecat halfing Chesterfield and Brenna manipulated into breaking into the store and planting the Orb of Thoth to poison Myrtle. For his troubles, Fish wound up being murdered by one of his own relatives, a claw-for-hire killer named Malcolm Ferguson.

We don't actually know where Ferguson murdered Fish, but he left the body propped up on the bench outside Chase's shop. The cover story we had to help promulgate was that Fish was involved in questionable online discussion sites and got himself mixed up with the wrong people.

I hated blackening the old guy's name like that, but no one needed to know the truth. Fish was trying to find a portal to get into Shevington because he believed if he could reach the Valley, he could shift into werecat form. His grandfather was a shifter, but he married a human. That left his offspring mentally unstable and perpetually caught between two worlds.

Because Mindy worked for us briefly, I knew Tori was right on the money when she said, "Those kids will buy anything with a whiff of ectoplasm about it and we have an ace in the hole — Darby. Let's send him in to convince them they don't have to go up in the mountains looking for a ghost because they have one right in their own house. That will give us time to get in and out of the Ionescu place without the junior ghost hunters under foot."

"I like it," I said, reaching for a fresh bear claw, my pastry vice of choice. "Let's talk to him now."

Tori held up her hand. "Hold on. I need to tell you that Festus and Rube are coming with us."

That stopped me mid-chew. When I could talk again, I said, "How the heck did that happen?"

"Apparently Festus was taking a nap under the counter when Cezar was here and heard the whole thing. He and Rube want to come along and 'case the joint.'"

She punctuated the last words with air quotes.

"Case the joint for *what*?"

"The two of them have been binge watching that show about the guys who go around buying junk. You know, *American Pickers*?" Tori explained. "Apparently Rube and his wrecking crew 'liberated' some old iron toys from a garage across town and they made a killing with them in an online auction."

"*Liberated?*" I said. "In other words, they stole them."

Tori shrugged helplessly. "I said the same thing, but the property has been abandoned for years so, as Festus put it, 'possession is nine-tenths of the law.' At least if we take them with us, they'll be casing a joint we have permission to case. Cezar isn't going to care if they take stuff out of the house. He wants the ghost gone."

"Okay," I said, "fine, but I intend to have a talk with Festus about his latest *entrepreneurial* efforts. While we're on the subject, what the heck does a werecat need money for anyway?"

"I wanted to know the same thing and he asked me if I had any idea what it was like to live with a tightwad like Chase."

As much as I hated to admit it, the old rascal was absolutely right. That was another aspect of Chase's personality that sometimes put us at cross-purposes — his ability to squeeze a dollar bill until Washington screamed for mercy.

"So," Tori continued, "what's the plan? When do we leave? I talked to Connor last night and he's excited. Things are quiet at the stables right now, so he can get away any time."

"I'm going to talk to Lucas tonight," I said, detailing my plan to take him to Tom's for a private dinner.

Tori approved wholeheartedly, especially when I explained I was embracing her "no magic" approach to the coming excursion.

"Now you're getting with the program!" she enthused. "I've already put together a list of things we need to order on Amazon."

Can I interject here that the words "need" and "Amazon" coming from Tori are usually an oxymoron?

She proceeded to show me a dizzying array of solar powered lanterns, collapsible stoves, freeze dried food, and something called a "LifeStraw" for safely drinking contaminated water.

As listing pages and prices swirled in my head, I called foul. "Get whatever you think we need," I said, holding my hands up in defeat. "I trust you. Just for heaven's sake make sure we have a way to brew coffee."

Tori looked wounded. "Jinksy, seriously? Do you think I'd take us out in the wilderness without the necessities of life?"

That's when I had to sit through an explanation of the hand-pumped espresso machine she planned to order.

"I thought this was supposed to be a camping trip," I said. "Aren't we going to be roughing it?"

"Well, yeah, but we don't have to be *uncomfortable* while we're doing it."

At that, we both burst out laughing. "I'm glad to hear you say that," I said, wiping my eyes, "because seriously, I haven't been enthusiastic about the word 'camping' since the moms shipped us off to Lake PleaseMakeItEnd that summer."

"That's not what it was called, that's just how you felt about it."

"If those people had made us roast one more marshmallow we'd have fallen into sugar comas," I declared with conviction. "I'm not the one who was almost kicked out of the place for putting a tarantula in my cabin mate's bed."

Tori's face darkened. "Loretta Lejean Longacker. I had almost forgotten about her. I hated to do that to a perfectly nice tarantula, but that girl needed to dial her attitude way down."

"Oh, you dialed it down for her alright. She spent the next week running to the counselor and crying every time a fly buzzed by. You probably put that poor girl into therapy for years."

"My sympathies to the therapist."

Since it was almost time to open for the day, I decided to put off talking to Darby until later. At lunchtime, I called him into the storeroom and first described the basket I needed for my dinner with Lucas that night. Then I explained what we wanted him to do with the HBH kids.

The brownie looked up at me with his earnest, wizened face and said, "Mistress, please do not ask me to scare someone."

Darby has a way of melting your heart whether he means to or not.

"You don't have to scare them, Darby. We need you to make them think they have a ghost in the house so they'll stay at home and investigate for a few days."

"How will I know what to do?"

Tori walked in and heard the question. "I can show you. Come to my place tonight. We'll have popcorn and watch ghost hunting videos on YouTube."

Darby's countenance brightened. "Oh, Mistress Tori! May I please bring Rodney and Glory and may we please have a slumber party?"

Whether that's what Tori intended or not, she said yes, which sent Darby blinking out to share the exciting news with his partners in crime.

"Thank you," I said. "I hope you didn't have other plans."

"Only a mirror call with Connor, but I can do that early. When you get in from your dinner with Lucas, tap on my door. The kids will be conked out by then. I'll come out so you can tell me everything."

The rest of the day crawled by. When I went down to the lair to get something out of my alcove, Greer assured me she'd gotten my message to Lucas. I went upstairs at 5 o'clock to change and check on the cats. They looked up from the couch in surprise when I walked in the door.

Now that they had the ability to come and go in the lair, they knew the daily routine by heart. If I hadn't come in, they'd have gone sauntering down their private staircase at 5:30, in time to be on hand for dinner.

While I had a strict rule about not giving my cats table scraps, there was nothing I could say when Darby started setting a cat-sized table for them complete with tablecloth, good china, and premier feline-appropriate main courses. The night before, their menu featured crab in a delicate cream broth with shrimp accents.

Yule let out with a vaguely alarmed, inquisitive "meow" that Xavier, Zeke, and Winston immediately echoed.

"Don't get your fur in a twist," I said. "You can go down to the lair without me. I have a date tonight."

Four pairs of eye whiskers shot up in surprise.

"That will be enough out of you. Go on, go down to the lair. I'll see you later."

Satisfied that their daily habits would not be infringed upon by my unruly behavior, the boys disappeared single file through the cat door followed by the sound of paws clunking on the stairs.

Free of eight prying eyes, I changed into a summery dress and went down to the espresso bar, fidgeting around in the store and trying not to watch the clock. I'd almost given up when the basement door opened and Lucas stepped out, trademark fedora in place, but wearing a dark suit instead of his usual rumpled clothes and battered leather duster.

"Wow," I said, "you clean up nice."

"As do you," he said, taking off his hat and bowing. "You look even prettier than usual tonight."

Dropping into a playful curtsy and using my best Scarlett O'Hara accent, I said, "Why thank you, kind sir."

With a flick of his wrist, Lucas sent his fedora flying toward the hat rack like a Frisbee. It snagged one of the hooks and settled neatly in place.

"So," he said, "what's the mystery? Where are we going tonight?"

Linking my arm through his, I said, "We are going to some place called the real world. Follow me."

Chapter Seven

Unlike my brother, Lucas did have previous experience with the human realm. That did nothing to diminish his fascination with my Prius. On the drive to Cotterville, he fiddled with the car's display, pulling up screens I'd never seen before.

Trying to concentrate on my driving, I said, "I wouldn't have taken you for a computer nerd. Magic pretty much blows every gadget on the market out of the water."

"That may be," he said, leaning back in his seat, "but inventions like this automobile are a kind of magic all their own. Humans spend a tremendous amount of their time trying to debunk things they regard as fantastical, all the while creating fantastical things."

"You do know I lived the first 30 years of my life as a human, right?"

Lucas grinned. "You still live your life as a human. You walk among the Fae and your control of magic continues to expand, but your heart and mind are grounded in this world."

A warning note sounded in my head. "Do you think that's a bad thing?"

"Not at all. It makes you quite unlike any Fae woman I've ever known."

The warning note morphed into a minor chord. I'll admit it. Lucas' casual references to women touched off a jealous reaction in me. The first time we placed a mirror call to Katrina Warner, the Witch of the Rowan, I didn't like the obvious familiarity with which she and Lucas greeted one another.

Later, when I learned they've been friends for years with no romantic entanglement involved, I felt ashamed of myself. After all, the man did have a life before he met me — a long life given that he's half Welsh water elf and half Druid.

When we pulled into the outskirts of Cotterville, Lucas watched the passing buildings with interest. It's a sleepy little southern town, like Briar Hollow, but he seemed to appreciate that the place has a special significance for me.

"You grew up here, right?"

"Yes. I lived and worked here until I inherited the store from Aunt Fiona. We're going to have dinner at the restaurant where I waited tables."

"Did I wear the right kind of clothes?" he asked. "Greer told me I shouldn't show up looking like 'a brigand from a cheap Hollywood theatrical production.'"

Laughing, I assured him that he looked quite handsome in his suit. "There won't be anyone else there. My former boss is letting me use the place for the evening. He's out of town for the week, and the diner is closed to the public."

That news sparked a special note of interest in Lucas' eyes. "That was nice of him. Since we don't have to be there at any specific time, would you mind showing me some of the town first? The sun is setting, and I'd enjoy seeing the locale in the daylight."

"Sure, I'll give you the grand tour."

Frankly, there aren't that many highlights, but I did the

whole guide thing, driving him around and talking about various "sites." Lucas asked questions and seemed particularly interested when I pulled up in front of the high school.

"Was it fun?" he asked, twisting his neck and taking in the building and adjacent sports fields.

"High school, fun? Parts of it were fun. Tori and I were in the band, and we worked in the school library. She blew up the chemistry lab one time, and I am still famous in town for turning a raccoon loose in the principal's office in protest after the guy axed the junior-senior banquet."

"Did you pay the raccoon?"

"Uh, I left him with half a dozen eggs and a pail of water."

"Don't tell that story to Rube," Lucas warned. "He gets sensitive about exploitation of raccoon labor."

"Well, in my defense, I never met a talking raccoon until Rube ran interference for me that day at the stables when I was trying to get a look at Connor."

"They're cagey. Humans have no appreciation for their intelligence. Raccoons are the only creatures I know that travel freely between all the realms. I couldn't do my job without access to the intricate network of connections Rube maintains. What did the raccoon do to the office?"

"He trashed it and escaped out a window the next morning. From the look of the place, he had a good time."

"They're artists of destruction. That's what makes them so effective as intelligence operatives. They leave the target in such total disarray their true goals are completely obscured. I have seen Rube and his guys do things to rooms that are beyond belief."

Our next stop was my childhood home, now owned by a new family. It pleased me to see a little girl riding her tricycle in the driveway, and I noted with approval the addition of a swing to the big hickory tree in the front yard.

"You don't miss it?" Lucas asked.

"No, not really. I have great memories, but it's fun having Mom and Dad two doors down. I love finding everyone in the lair at the end of the day waiting for Darby to serve supper. Honestly, I consider the fairy mound to be my family home now. If you've seen enough, we can go on to the diner."

"Sounds great. Thanks for the tour."

I took the back streets to Tom's, pulling into my old parking spot at the rear of the building. My key turned smoothly in the lock and we walked through the kitchen. In the deserted dining room, Lucas let out a low whistle.

"This is amazing," he said, pivoting to take in the long counter fronted with backless red stools trimmed in chrome that matched the booths along the opposite wall. "I haven't seen a diner like this since the Fifties. Is there one of those boxes with the music plates in them?"

"A jukebox? It's right over there."

"Do you have any of the coins that will make it play?"

"Better than that, I know where Tom keeps his bucket of spare change."

Lucas frowned. "How can you keep change in a bucket? Change is a dynamic process of life."

"Not that kind of change," I laughed. "Haven't you ever used human money?"

"The paper variety, yes."

"Change is the coins you get back when the paper money equals more than the price of the thing you're paying for."

Reaching behind the counter, I came up with a coffee can full of quarters, which I rattled to illustrate my definition.

I joined him in front of the jukebox, feeding coins into the slot. Tom keeps nothing but ancient country tunes stocked in the machine, so I picked Patsy Cline, Johnny Cash, and some Merle Haggard.

When the opening notes of "I Fall to Pieces" began to play,

Lucas' face lit up. "I know this song!" he said, holding his hand out to me. "May I have this dance?"

Surprised, but delighted, I took his hand and stepped into his arms. I don't know what I expected, but he executed a credible, if somewhat dated, two-step. To my pleasure, Lucas proved to be a strong lead.

"Where on earth did you learn to two-step?" I asked.

"Nashville. There was an incident there in the 1950s that required my attention. I was looking for a rogue leprechaun who was working in disguise at the major music venue in town. He played a rather interesting instrument, something called a steel guitar."

That literally stopped me in my tracks. "A leprechaun played steel guitar at the Opry?"

"He did. He found the sequined costumes exceedingly attractive."

"When I worked here if you'd told me a story like that I'd have taken you for an escapee from the nearest insane asylum."

I was still standing in the circle of his arms, my hands resting lightly on the lapels of his suit. The fact that I was making no attempt to move wasn't lost on Lucas.

"Not that I'm not enjoying myself," he said, "but what are we doing here?"

"Well, when I unpack that basket you carried in for me, we're going to have dinner. I wanted us to come some place where we could talk by ourselves."

"What are we going to talk about?"

"I thought it was time we got to know each other better."

Even absent the fedora for a prop, the grin Lucas gave me was rakish and faintly suggestive. "I thought we got to know each other pretty well that night on the wall in Shevington."

At the mention of our first kiss, I felt my cheeks grow warm. "That was certainly a good start."

"It was," he said, "but you still had feelings for Chase. Has that changed?"

My fingers smoothed the dark fabric of his suit. "It has," I said, keeping my eyes on the red silk tie knot resting between the white wings of his shirt collar.

"Let me see your eyes when you say that," Lucas commanded softly.

Raising my gaze to meet his, I said, "I don't have those kind of feelings for Chase anymore. I do have them for you."

The first time he kissed me, Lucas tasted like chocolate. This time, there was the faintest suggestion of salt on his lips, something I now understand is part of his water elf heritage. He left me breathless, and a little dazed.

"No thoughts of Chase MacGregor?" he asked when our lips parted.

"Who?" I whispered before I claimed his mouth again.

Dinner turned out to be late. In fact, the whole evening ran longer than I'd imagined when I planned our date. It certainly never occurred to me that things would go so well. We didn't slip back into the store until some time after one in the morning.

When Lucas kissed me again at the door to the basement and told me good night, I felt a pang of longing as he closed the door behind him. I don't imagine he'd taken three steps down toward the lair before the door to Tori's micro apartment opened.

"Young lady," she whispered dramatically, in an all-to-convincing impersonation of my mother, "do you know what time it is?"

That got her nothing but a silly laugh from me. Grabbing my arm and dragging me into the light falling through her doorway, Tori took one look at my dreamy-eyed expression and said, "Espresso bar. Now. Tell me everything."

I followed her to one of the tables and sat down. "Are Darby and the others asleep?" I asked.

"Sawing logs."

"Did Darby get any good haunting ideas on YouTube?"

Tori plopped down across from me and groaned. "Not really. He spent most of his time hiding his face or asking why the ghosts were being so mean. I finally put on *The Little Mermaid* and told him we'd talk tomorrow. So come on, what happened?"

"There was driving and talking and dancing and kissing," I babbled. "Followed by eating and talking and more dancing and more kissing."

"Wow! I haven't seen you this moonstruck since high school, and this was a real date, outside the fairy mound, no magic involved."

On that point, I had to correct her.

"Oh, there was magic involved," I sighed, "just not the kind requiring Fae powers."

For the record, that wasn't a statement I would be able to make again for some time to come.

Chapter Eight

D arby stood in front of me with his arms crossed defiantly over his chest. "Mistress, all the ghosts I know are *nice*. The ones on YouTube are awful and mean. I won't be like that even if you order me to do it."

Since I've never ordered Darby to do anything, we were dealing with a fair amount of brownie drama, but that didn't lessen our diminutive friend's level of upset.

I looked over at Tori for an explanation. "What the heck did you show him last night anyway?"

"It wasn't my fault," she said defensively. "I went into the kitchen to make popcorn, and he clicked a link for 'black-eyed children.'"

When the statement didn't register a reaction from me, Tori shook her head. "You are so culturally illiterate sometimes it isn't even funny."

She took out her smartphone, thumb-typed for a second, and then handed the device to me. The screen displayed a Wikipedia article with the disturbing image of a little boy with jet black eyes. Scanning the text, phrases jumped out at me like *urban legend, paranormal creatures, age 6 to 16, show up on residential doorsteps.*

Looking down at Darby, I said, "I don't blame you. I'd have been creeped out, too."

"Thank you, Mistress," he sniffed, putting on an air of wounded, dignity. He shot Tori a look of triumphant vindication. "I knew Mistress *Jinx* would understand."

When Tori stuck her tongue out at him, I said, "Alright children, play nice. Let's try this again."

I pulled out two chairs from the nearest table and asked Darby to sit with me. He complied, but suspicion still clouded his wrinkled features. Don't ever tell him I said so, but Darby looks like a beardless garden gnome. We don't, however, use the "g" word with him unless we have time for a lengthy, indignant lecture on the differences in brownies, gnomes, and dwarves.

"That video you saw isn't what we're asking you to do at all," I said. "We want you to go into Mindy, Kyle, and Nick's house using your power of invisibility and make them think they have a ghost by doing simple things. Make sounds, like knocking, that they can't identify. Maybe move something slowly across the floor or even pick something up, so they think the object is levitating."

Tori chimed in. "They'll probably use a gadget called a K2 meter to see if they can detect your presence. All it does is measure spikes in electricity. I can rig up something you can put in your pocket that you can trigger to make the K2 light up. That will keep them busy for hours."

Darby drew his brows together in concentration. "I do not have to make my eyes black? It makes for a most unattractive visage."

He wasn't going to get an argument from me on that one. "Agreed. No black eyes."

When he still appeared indecisive, Tori suggested a compromise.

"How about this? Go over there tonight for a test run. We'll put a headset on you so we can talk to you and send one of the GNATS drones to give us a video feed. That way we can coach you on what to do. If you hate it, we'll let you off the hook and come up with another plan."

Darby's eyes widened in alarm. "I am to be on a hook?"

"No, no, *no*," I said hastily, patting his arm comfortingly. "That's a phrase humans use to indicate someone is obligated to do something. What she means is that if you don't like pretending to be a ghost, we won't make you do it."

That seemed to mollify him because he agreed to the plan, but not without reproachful glances in Tori's direction.

With those high-level negotiations completed, we finished our coffee in peace and opened the store on time. Sometime around nine o'clock, the UPS guy came in the back door with his arms full of boxes.

"Hey Tori!" he called out. "You've got a real haul today. It's gonna take me more than one trip."

"No problem, Rick," she called back. "I'll have your mocha ready when you're finished."

Being on a first-name basis with the UPS man *might* be the first sign of online shopping addiction. Plying him with hot chocolate drinks, on the other hand, is a dead giveaway.

The guy hadn't exaggerated. It took six trips to amass an impressive pile of packages outside the door to Tori's apartment. I waited until he'd collected his mocha and left to drag her off to one side. "What on *earth* did you order?"

"You told me to get what I thought we'd need for our camping trip. This is the stuff I thought we'd need."

Rolling my eyes, I said, "You do know that we're camping in the mountains outside of town — in a house, no less — not in the Yukon?"

"You said you didn't want to be uncomfortable. I was only keeping your best interests in mind."

Those big, innocent eyes she flashed in my direction didn't make me feel better until she ripped open a box and pulled out a portable power station the size of an ice chest followed by the hand-pump espresso maker.

I shut up. Electrical power *and* high-quality caffeine — we were getting off to a good start.

As she sorted through her purchases and made piles of sleeping bags, LED lanterns, freeze-dried food pouches, and a collapsible fire pit, I went back to work. We might kill ourselves lugging all that stuff up to the house, but once we got there, we'd be fully equipped for almost anything.

That evening, Darby insisted on setting out a supper buffet before he went to the Pike house. I sent Rube along to ride shotgun.

Before they left, I motioned Rube over to where I was sitting with Greer by the fireplace. "If he gets into any trouble, create a distraction and get him out of there."

"No worries, Doll. The coon is on the case," Rube assured me. "Distraction is my middle name."

Greer sighed. "Reuben, your middle name is Eugene."

"Figure of speech, Red," he said, lapsing into pig Latin. "And ix-nay on the iddle-may ame-nay."

The baobhan sith answered him in real Latin. I can't be sure, but I think she warned him not to screw this assignment up or his middle name would be broadcast to every raccoon bar in North America. Darby inspires protective instincts in all of us.

"Is your headset working?" I asked Rube.

He put a black paw up to his ear. "Mother Goose, Mother Goose, this is Psycho Wombat. We five by five?"

Through my earpiece I heard Tori say, "Roger that, Psycho Wombat."

I looked down at the grinning raccoon. "*Psycho Wombat?*"

"Best code name *ever*," he enthused, punctuating the sentiment with a vigorous paw pump. "I'm not using anything else from now on. That dame Tori is a freaking genius of covert ops."

Darby stood waiting on the landing for Rube with a slightly scared, thoroughly worried expression.

As the raccoon waddled up the steps, I held my hand out to the brownie, who grasped my fingers tightly. "You are going to do *great*," I assured him. "Have fun with it."

"I will try, mistress," he said, blinking into invisibility. "But I do not think I am cut out for work under the covers."

Willing myself not to laugh, I corrected him. "Undercover work."

"That either," he replied mournfully as his voice trailed off up the steps.

Once the two of them were in the alley, the video feed on the big screen TV sprang to life. "GNATS 1 to Mother Goose," the pilot said, "we have visual on the team."

"Stay close GNATS 1," Tori ordered. "We need eyes on the asset inside the target destination."

"Copy that, Mother Goose."

I felt like I'd been plunked down into a twisted plot where James Bond meets Walt Disney with a side order of *Guardians of the Galaxy*.

Festus jumped up on the arm of my chair. "I'm telling you," he said, idly scratching his whiskers, "I thank the Universe every day I don't have a butt like a raccoon."

"Have you taken a good look at that pouch hanging off your gut?" I asked.

The werecat sniffed indignantly. "My belly fur is quite lush."

"Two of those words are accurate," I shot back. "Belly and lush."

Arching an eye whisker, Festus said, "Let she who is without Spanx cast the first stone."

You see? There are good reasons why I don't like my cats associating with Festus. Too much information sharing.

As we all watched, Rube expertly led the still invisible Darby through alleyways and side streets until they slipped into the front yard of the Pike house.

Static rippled over the coms unit. "We are in position and good for incursion."

On cue, Tori picked up the phone and called Joe's Taco Takeout. "Hi. I need an order of two dozen tacos delivered to 632 Maple. I'd like to pay by credit card. Fifteen minutes? Fantastic."

"Two dozen?" Chase asked. "Isn't that going overboard?"

"You obviously don't know anything about the appetite of millennials," Tori said. "I probably should have ordered *three* dozen."

While we waited for the delivery to arrive, Beau broached a topic he'd already raised earlier in the evening.

"It would be quite a simple matter for me to arrange for one or more denizens of the cemetery to take on this assignment. Perhaps having an actual ghost performing the haunting would lead to more reliable results."

He sounded mildly offended.

"Not a chance," I replied, in a tone that indicated the topic was not up for further discussion. "After that disastrous baseball game video, there is no way I am willing to risk the HBH kids getting more footage of authentic spooks. Darby will be fine as soon as he understands what we need him to do."

Since Beau and Tori were jointly responsible for the events that facilitated the capturing of that video — which went viral, I might add — neither of them argued with me. Duke, who was featured prominently in the finished product ducked under Beau's desk with a repentant whine. Smart dog.

"There's the delivery guy," Festus said. "How come he's never that punctual when *I* order tacos?"

"Probably because you don't tip," I said.

"Hey!" Festus protested. "Do you see pockets in this suit?"

As we watched the screen, the driver knocked on the door. When Kyle answered, the guy held out the bag and said, "Two dozen regulars, right?"

"Uh, Dude, you've got the wrong house."

Checking his clipboard, the delivery man said, "Is this 632 Maple?"

"Yeah."

"Right address and they're paid for. Either you take'em and eat'em or I throw'em away. I'm not allowed to bring'em back to the shop. Shame to waste good food."

Kyle took the tacos.

As he closed the door, we assumed Darby slipped inside because the GNATS drone entered the house as well. Over the coms unit, Rube said. "They're in. Assuming observation post."

"What's your position, Psycho Wombat?" Tori asked.

"Front porch window, Mother Goose. Direct line of sight on the action."

Still standing in the foyer of the house, Kyle called out. "Guys! Free tacos!"

We heard the sound of feet pounding down the stairs, and Nick came into view. "Free?" he asked. "What's up with that?"

"He had our address, and they're paid for," Kyle said. "Let's eat!"

Mindy was already in the living room sitting cross-legged on the floor with her laptop resting on the coffee table. She shoved the computer aside to make room for the take-out bag while Kyle went into the kitchen for paper plates and sodas.

The three settled down to their meal, chowing down enthusiastically and discussing plans for their next excursion to the house owned by the Ionescus.

"I don't know," Nick said, crunching thoughtfully. "We were up there all night last time and didn't get anything useful, plus those creepy guys who work for the owner showed up and kicked us out. That light in the attic could have been a reflection from the highway. I think we need to find a better location. You know, one that isn't posted 'No Trespassing?'"

As Mindy and Kyle started to argue with him, I said, "Get Darby in there."

"What do you want me to tell him to do?" Tori asked.

"I don't know. Be creative."

She chewed on her lip for a minute and then said, "Darby, pick up a taco."

There was a pause, and then a single taco rose off the table and hung suspended in mid-air. The effect on the HBH kids was immediate and dramatic. Mindy tried to back up but was stopped by the couch, which she wound up climbing until she tumbled over the back.

Nick dropped his taco and knocked his Coke over, but Kyle had presence enough of mind to grab his camera.

Bingo.

With his free hand, he slapped Kyle on the back. "Man, *wake up!* Get the K2."

Kyle reached for a backpack and brought out a gray plastic box with what looked like a meter on top.

"Darby," Tori said, "hit the switch."

The taco wobbled and then the light on the K2 meter shot up to red. All three kids let out a shout of elation, which must have startled Darby because he dropped the taco, but it didn't matter. We had the HBH kids right where we wanted them.

Later that evening, when Darby and Rube got back to the lair, the brownie hit me full in the chest. I returned the hug as he cried, "Oh, Mistress! You did not tell me we would make them happy. I will pretend to be a ghost for as long as you wish me to play the part."

"You don't have to do it for long," I said. "Just while we're up in the mountains. Rube is coming with us. Are you okay doing this on your own?"

From across the room, Beau made a magnanimous offer. "I will undertake to instruct Darby, and if he wishes, to accompany him. I can ensure that my presence will not be detected."

"Thank you, Beau," I said. "I won't worry about Darby if you're looking out for him."

If I had offended Beau by my refusal to use a real ghost for the assignment, my friend got over it as soon as he saw Darby's happiness.

"So," Tori said, looking at me expectantly, "are we good to go?"

"We are good to go. Let the camping begin."

Chapter Nine

Early the next morning, Connor came through the basement door about 7 o'clock. We were sitting in the espresso bar with the moms, Greer, and Brenna. The quartet would be in charge while we were out of town. With their combination of powers and experience, I had no doubt they could handle anything that came up — including the possible reappearance of Irenaeus Chesterfield.

The third time I went through the list I'd drawn up for them, Mom gave me *the look*. "Norma Jean, Gemma and I were practicing magic before you were born, and Brenna has been at it since . . . "

"The 12th century," Brenna supplied helpfully and with no small degree of bemusement.

Greer chimed in. "While I do not care to disclose my precise age, I will say that I somewhat predate Brenna. I believe we are quite equipped to run a store in a backwater rural town for a few days."

Connor burst out laughing. "Give it up, Sis. You're outclassed."

He bent and gave mom a kiss on the cheek before hugging me and catching hold of Tori's hand. She pulled him into the empty chair next to her and didn't let go, entwining their fingers in full sight of the moms, who exchanged an "I told you so" look, but otherwise didn't miss a beat.

"So," Mom said, "if you are quite done treating us like incompetent children, get out of here already."

"*Harrumph*," I groused. "You don't have to gang up on me just because I'm thorough."

"A thorough fussbudget is more like it," Mom said. "Connor, get these two on the road."

The basement door opened right on cue. Festus and Rube sauntered through followed by Lucas who was carrying his backpack and two smaller ones I assumed belonged to the furry members of our expedition.

I have to admit my heart did a little flip-flop at the sight of my DGI agent. He'd switched out his fedora for a vaguely Australian leather hat that sat on his head at the usual roguish angle — with the addition of Rodney perched atop the crown.

Lucas and I exchanged a wordless greeting with sufficient electricity that everyone in the room noticed.

Festus' head swiveled to look at Lucas, and then shifted toward me as his whiskers curled in a grin. "Well, well, *well*," he drawled. "About damned time."

While I have no doubt Festus gave Chase a sympathetic ear in the wake of our break up, I also knew the old werecat was relieved. Festus understood both sides of the situation—the attraction, and the consequences.

Beside him, Rube frowned, "What? I miss something?" He looked at me and then back at Lucas before the light dawned. "Oh! *Suh-wheet!*"

I blushed. Lucas blushed. Rodney shot me a thumbs up, and everyone started laughing.

Lucas shrugged. "Guess we don't have to make an announcement."

"Guess not," I agreed, "but let's get out of here before I die of embarrassment."

That touched off more laughter, as we started carting stuff out to my Prius. Do not underestimate the hauling capacity of the trendy hybrid. We packed everything in the back and still had room for Festus and Rube to claim a rectangle of space behind the backseat where they immediately started a game of blackjack.

I drove, with Rodney curled around my neck. Lucas rode up front with me, while Tori and Connor claimed the backseat. Everything seemed to be going according to plan. Little did I know, however, that back in the store a plot was being hatched, with my mother as the ringleader.

"ARE THEY GONE?"

"Yep," Gemma said, closing the apartment door behind her and rejoining the other women in the espresso bar. "I watched them from Tori's bedroom window until they were out of the alley and down the street."

"Good," Kelly said. "We don't have to open the store for another hour. More than enough time to discuss what I'm proposing."

Greer stood up and walked behind the counter. "I sense more coffee to be in order. Anyone else?"

"I'll take another cup," Brenna said, going to join her.

"Bring more bear claws while you're over there," Gemma said, reclaiming her chair.

"Gemma," Kelly scolded, "what are you thinking? You never eat more than one pastry."

"I never eat more than one pastry in front of the girls,"

Gemma corrected her. "It's just us old ladies now, and this is definitely going to be a two-pastry conversation."

Brenna and Greer returned with steaming cups of coffee and a platter of confections.

"Shouldn't Myrtle be here," Greer asked, "or are you hiding this information from her as well?"

Kelly shook her head. "On my best day I'm not that sneaky. Myrtle knows what I want to do and agrees that at this stage, at least, involving the girls would only complicate matters. You may have noticed that my daughter can occasionally get worked up."

"Am I to assume," Brenna said, "that Greer and I are included in this conversation because we have a higher tolerance for complications?"

Kelly laughed and put her hand on Brenna's arm. "You're included in this conversation because you're a member of our coven, and both of you are family. But, yes, I don't think what I'm going to say will freak you out the way it would Jinx."

The baobhan sith inclined her head in acknowledgment. "You do me a great honor. My own family long ago cast me out for my work with the DGI, but familial status or not, I don't think Jinx will be pleased with any of us for going behind her back."

"Leave Norma Jean to me," Kelly said firmly. "Now, ladies, here is what I propose. Working together, we find a way to enter the sealed cavern Chesterfield used as his base. Seraphina and Ioana are still in there, chained in their caskets. I wouldn't wish a fate like that on my worst enemies. I want to get them out of the cavern and turn them over to the Ionescus for proper disposal."

Greer and Brenna regarded her with stunned silence. The baobhan sith recovered first.

"Am I to understand that you want to release two *Strigoi mort blasfematoare*? Have you lost your mind?"

"Not release," Kelly said. "We'll leave them chained in their caskets and take them to their people."

"Who will kill them," Greer said.

"That's better than leaving them trapped in those coffins for eternity," Kelly replied.

Greer turned to Gemma. "You are in agreement with this madness?"

Gemma shrugged. "Whether I agree or disagree, Kelly has it in her head to do this thing. In all the years we've known each other, we always go over the cliff together. If she's in, I'm in."

Brenna cleared her throat. "Would someone please explain to me how two *Strigoi mort blasfematoare* came to be imprisoned by Irenaeus in a cavern in North Carolina?"

"Oh," Kelly said, "sorry. Let me see if I can give you the short version."

After going over the details of the original car accident in which Seraphina and Ioana were killed, she explained how Anton Ionescu used their deaths as a pretext to exile Connor in Shevington.

"When Jinx worked the bit of magic that freed you from Knasgowa's grave, she awakened the girls by accident," Kelly finished.

Brenna's brow furrowed. "They were not properly staked and beheaded after the car accident?"

"Anton couldn't bring himself to do it," Gemma said. "When they rose from their crypt, he tried to keep them under wraps, but they got away from him and wound up more or less working for Chesterfield."

"Ah," Brenna said, "an opportunity Irenaeus would not pass up. Undoubtedly the girls defied him in some way, and he chose to punish them, but how do you know they are in the cavern?"

"Chesterfield kidnapped my son," Kelly said. "It's a long

story, but Connor was able to escape. Once we knew he was safe, Jinx sent a GNATS drone to penetrate as far into the mountain as possible. They're so tiny, they can work their way through cracks and crevices in the stone. The pilot got close enough to look into the cavern. The caskets were clearly visible on the video. So what do you say? Are you in?"

Brenna looked at Greer. "We cannot let them attempt this without our assistance."

"Well," the baobhan sith replied with resignation, "never let it be said that a MacVicar woman is not prepared to go over a cliff with her friends. I'm in."

"I am 'in' as well," Brenna said, "but if I may venture to ask, how do you suggest we remove the caskets from a sealed cavern?"

Kelly toyed with the rim of her coffee cup. "That is where things could get a little sticky and where you come in. I want you to direct us in merging our powers to dematerialize the caskets from the interior of the cave to the outside. You're the only one of us with the experience to try something like that."

"Brenna's experience notwithstanding," Greer said levelly, "you do understand that there's a good chance we will fail and imprison the girls in the stone of the mountain . . ."

"Or that our magic will be attracted to their life source," Brenna added, "and we will bring only the Strigoi to the outside free of their bindings . . . "

"Or that we could collapse the interior of the cave and start a landslide," Gemma chimed in.

Kelly set her mouth in a disapproving line. "We are four powerful, magical practitioners and as we just explained to the girls, the two of you have been at this for centuries. I think we can overcome a few minor potential hiccups."

"Famous last words," Gemma said, draining her cup and slamming it down on the table. "Come on ladies, we have stores to open. We can knock down mountains and set vampire hordes loose later."

Brenna laughed, "Two Strigoi do not a horde make."

"Don't be so sure about that," Gemma warned her. "You haven't met Seraphina and Ioana."

Chapter Ten

When we reached our destination, Lucas got out and unlocked the gate with the keys Cezar sent to the shop. I drove through and waited while Lucas resecured the chain. Instead of getting back in the car, he motioned for me to roll the window down.

"We should park here and hike up to the house. If the HBH kids spot a car on the slope, they might decide to come check it out."

I didn't relish the idea of playing pack mule, but I also didn't like the look of the rutted, overgrown lane that disappeared into the forest. With Lucas directing me, I pulled behind a small copse of trees and thick brush. To my surprise, he produced a camouflage tarp from the luggage in the back.

After we unloaded our gear, Lucas threw the tarp over the bright red car completely obscuring it from view — so completely, I suspected the tarp benefited from an enchantment. Since Tori didn't bring up the infraction of the "rules" neither did I, but I did wonder if Lucas had any other surprises planned.

Satisfied that the Prius couldn't be seen from the road, we

divided the supplies for the hike. I reached for the pack with the mesh panels we used to accommodate Festus' lame hip.

"Oh," Rube said sarcastically, "so that's how it works. Mr. High and Mighty rides and the underprivileged raccoon has to walk."

"Benefits of seniority," Festus said with smug satisfaction.

"Seniority?" Rube said. "Ah, I get it! You're too old to walk."

Rube knew perfectly well Festus couldn't make the hike with his lame hip, but he didn't know that if the werecat shifted into his big cat form, he'd be able to manage the trail without a problem. A glimmering ripple of energy washed over the ginger cat, leaving a thickly muscled mountain lion standing in his place.

"You were saying?" Festus snarled.

Rube gulped. "Beautiful day for a walk, huh, buddy?"

"That's more like it," Festus purred. "I wasn't looking forward to picking striped fur out of my teeth."

The raccoon took a step back, but Rodney moved forward confidently and pointed to Festus' back.

"You want a lift?" Festus asked.

When the rat nodded, Festus stretched out his right front leg. Rodney scampered up fearlessly and settled between the old cat's ears. He promptly shot Rube a self-satisfied smirk.

"Guess I didn't get the memo about National Disrespect the Raccoon Day, Rube grumbled. Even his rodentialness is taking pot shots at me."

Then he spotted all of us grinning at him. Nice support from the bipeds," he groused. "Can we get a move on already?"

Lucas looked at me. "Which way?"

"Cezar said if we decided to walk in, we should follow the tree line until we get to a small creek. About a hundred yards upstream we'll find a path that leads to the house."

As we started across the meadow, Lucas fell in beside me

while Connor and Tori walked side by side. Festus limped along at the back of the group while Rube waddled off to the side mostly obscured by the tall grass.

My muscles loosened up with each stride. I turned my face toward the warm sunlight and let the bird songs erase any thoughts of "civilization."

"Feels good to be outside, doesn't it?" Lucas asked.

"It does. Sometimes I forget how much time we spend in the store or down in the lair. How about you? Do you get outdoors much?"

In the wake of our date to Tom's, I realized how little Lucas and I knew about one another. I hoped we'd be able to start filling the information gap on this trip.

"It depends on the assignment," he said, shifting the pack on his back. "If I'm going after some Fae smuggler, I could be in the middle of the Sahara or rummaging through the basement of the Smithsonian. Depends on how the target operates."

I knew the load Lucas was carrying had to be heavy. He drew the short straw and got to lug the big battery pack, but nothing about the DGI agent's demeanor suggested he was straining.

"What do Fae smugglers have to do with protecting the integrity of the Grid?" I asked.

"You shouldn't take the name of the agency literally. We do protect the Trees, but we also do what they tell us to do. If one of the Mother Trees says an artifact needs to be retrieved, we go after the artifact. No questions asked. I mean seriously, you and I met because the Mother Oak wanted me to stop you from seeing Connor."

Over his shoulder, Connor said, "I'm still annoyed about that, by the way."

"Be annoyed at Rube, not at me," Lucas countered. "He's the one who ran interference for her that day."

From the tall grass, the raccoon said, "And it's a good thing I did. Not meaning no insult, Jinx, stealth ain't your thing. If anybody cares, I smell water."

We all stopped talking and listened. The sound of a bubbling stream came from somewhere to our left. The group changed course and quickly found the creek. We stepped out of the bright sunshine and into the dense forest shade on rocky ground that sloped upward.

As promised, we found a rough trail that wound back and forth on itself. The path had been laid out to manage the ascent on a gentle grade. What could have been a precarious hike, turned into a pleasant walk through the trees. A few disgruntled squirrels protested our invasion of their home territory, and we startled a whitetail buck, but otherwise, we were completely alone.

After 20 minutes, the path stopped at the base of a set of rock steps. At the top, we found a ragged clearing. The abandoned farmhouse sat at an angle to the road far below, the front of the house facing the woods to our left.

At one time, the place must have been a prosperous home. There were chimneys on both sides and a large, railed porch. Gabled windows jutted out prominently on the second story, and the roof sported a sagging weathervane.

Most of the white paint had peeled away from the structure exposing gray, weathered wood, but I could see remnants of green trim on the windows. Thick tendrils of kudzu covered the wide steps and blocked our access to the front door.

I looked at Tori. "Come on, don't we get a kudzu exemption for the use of magic?"

"Nope," she said firmly. "That's why we brought the menfolk along."

Shrugging out of his pack, Connor said, "I knew this invitation had to be too good to be true. Come on, Lucas. We have work to do."

"A DGI agent is never unprepared," Lucas replied, taking off his own pack. He dug in a side pocket and produced two wicked looking machetes. Tossing one to Connor, Lucas hefted the other. "Shall we?"

"We shall," Connor agreed.

Festus let out a bored yawn. "While you humans take care of the lawn work, I'm going to rest my eyes."

He padded lazily over to a large sun puddle, circled the spot a time or two and settled down for his nap. Rodney, who had ridden all the way up the mountain on the old cat's head, scurried toward me. I bent down and scooped him up, holding him at eye level.

"There are hawks in these mountains," I said. "When we're outdoors, you have to be inside somebody's collar. Do you understand?"

Nodding earnestly, Rodney ran up my arm and into the neck of my shirt. I felt the tickle of his whiskers against my skin as he positioned himself to have a good view of everything going on around him.

Rube stood up on his hind legs and surveyed the old house. "If you folks will excuse me," he said, cracking his knuckles with a look of happy expectation on his face, "I got me some breaking and entering to do."

With that, he waddled to the side of the porch and dove head first into the kudzu. We heard him rattling around, saw an overgrown rocking chair move, and then watched the front door swing inward on protesting hinges.

Rube's black-masked face popped through the vines. "I'm gonna do a recon run while you bipeds weed whack. Catch you on the inside." He disappeared without another word.

Lucas, machete in hand, looked at Tori. "Still no on the magic?"

"Still no on the magic."

"Okay," he said, drawing back the blade. "Stand clear." He

gave a mighty swing with one hand and pulled back a mass of vines with the other.

Beside him, Connor replicated the motion. The two of them fell into an efficient rhythm. To help out, Tori and I started dragging the cast-off foliage to the side. The growth was so thick, the guys worked for almost an hour, sweat pouring off their faces to clear our path into the house.

When they were done, Tori handed each of them a cold bottle of water from her insulated pack. Curious, I pulled back the flap and looked inside. Neat stacks of food containers stared back at me.

"Dare I hope that's lunch?"

"You dare. I figured we'd have a fire and do the whole cooking thing tonight, so I brought cold stuff for lunch."

Wiping at his brow, Connor said, "Cold is good. When do we eat?"

"Now," I said. "Picnic first, then explore."

Chapter Eleven

Tori spread a second tarp under the shade of an impressive oak. The gnarled, aged branches made me think of the Mother Tree in Shevington. This oak, however, didn't speak to us in cryptic phrases or offer sage advice on how to proceed with our lives.

Don't get me wrong, I love the Mother Tree, but sometimes she can be a . . . well, overbearing . . . in a thoroughly sweet, parental way. Imagine a helicopter mother to the power of ten thousand — with leaves.

Even though I hadn't done a fraction of the work Lucas and Connor put in, getting out of the sun felt deliciously cool and relaxing. Tori produced more cold water, a beautiful bowl of sliced fruit, and thick chicken salad sandwiches on home-made, buttered bread. She even thought to bring a pecan pie for dessert.

After he finished his second sandwich, my brother stretched out on his back and closed his eyes. "Can't we explore after we have a nap?" he asked, already sounding half asleep.

Festus licked his whiskers and blinked. "Finally, someone with half a brain. I'm in on the nap plan."

"Don't even think about it you two," Tori said. "We have to check out the house and figure out where we're going to set up for the night. Someone needs to assemble the fire pit and gather wood . . ."

Before she could finish her growing "to do" list, a gray streak shot out the front door of the house complete with frantic sound effects. The only phrases I could make out were "what the hell" and "don't freaking touch me."

Rube skidded to a stop in front of us with every hair on his body sticking straight up. Regarding us with wild eyes, he said, "That dump is seriously off the charts weird. Something *petted* me."

All heads swiveled toward the open door. I, for one, half expected a marauding monster to charge out after the distraught raccoon.

"What was it?" Lucas asked, getting to his feet and settling his hat in place like a piece of battle armor.

"How in the name of the Trash Gods should I know?" Rube said. "One minute I'm minding my own business looking through this big ole roll top desk and the next something's touching me."

Minding his own business, huh? To me it sounded more like he'd been pilfering and the resident ghost objected.

"What did it look like?" Lucas persisted. "The thing that touched you."

"You. Are. Not. *Listening*," Rube said. "It didn't look like nothing. I was alone in the room, sitting in the desk chair. The hair on my arm went like flat and something touched me. I didn't stick around and ask no questions."

If there was any doubt that we were sent here to deal with a haunting, Rube's story settled the matter.

Tori was already repacking the leftover food. Connor was sitting up fully awake. The only member of our party who looked disinterested — shock of shocks — was Festus. The werecat stood up, stretched, and ambled over to Rube, proceeding to sniff his fur.

"*Hey!*" Rube roared. "Ain't you getting a little personal there, McGregor?"

"Did you know," Festus said conversationally, "that the feline sense of smell is fourteen times stronger than a dog's? You know what you smell like?"

"What?" Rube asked uneasily.

"A raccoon who spends too much time in the sewer."

I won't bother to tell you the words they exchanged after that. In general, I try not to use that kind of language. Finally, Lucas and I both had enough. He grabbed Rube by the scruff of the neck and I dragged Festus off to one side by the ear.

"You do know I'm a mountain lion, right?" Festus said, glaring at me through slitted eyes, his offended ear twitching in annoyance.

"Don't *even*. You're a mountain lion sworn to defend me, so ditch the tough cat act. While we're on the subject, do you really have to stay in your big cat form while we're up here? If I didn't know better, I'd say you were trying to intimidate Rube."

Festus sniffed indignantly. "I'm not *trying* to intimidate anyone. I'm naturally intimidating. At most, I will confess to yanking his striped tail for the entertainment value. As for why I'm in this form, you hit the nail on the head. I have a responsibility to protect you. I can do a better job of that when I'm big enough to put up a convincing fight."

"Okay, fine," I said, "I get it and thanks, by the way, but will you lay off Rube? He's excitable on a good day."

"Flaw of the species, but yeah, I'll cut him a little slack."

Finally, a concession. "Thank you. Now, did you smell anything unusual on him?"

The fur between his amber eyes furrowed. "I'm not sure.

He does smell like a raccoon and there really is a hint of Eau d' Sewer there. You ever try to get methane out of your fur?"

"Can't say I have. What aren't you telling me?"

"Whatever else I detected was faint, but the odor wasn't anything I've encountered before. Maybe it was something Rube brushed up against inside the house."

That was a convenient explanation — maybe too convenient. "Have you picked up odors from ghosts before?"

The werecat shook his head. "Never, Ectoplasm doesn't have a scent."

From behind me I heard Lucas say, "I'll put you down if you'll straighten up and get in a better mood. What the heck is up with you today anyway?"

He was holding Rube at arm's length. The raccoon's fists were balled up and he was flailing at empty air.

"You get *petted* by some freaking ghost and tell me how you like it. Not to mention McGregor cheats at blackjack the same way he cheats at poker. He took fifty bucks off me on the way up here. Now put me *down* already."

"Reuben," Lucas warned. "A bad attitude will get you nowhere. Try again."

Rube stopped fighting and made a visible effort at self-control. "Fine!" he hissed through gritted teeth, "I'm calm already. Now put me *down!*"

"Hold on," I said. "Keep him there for a minute. Festus, were you cheating at blackjack?"

The werecat made a sour face. "Only to get back at him over that poker incident the other day."

"When you were also cheating," I pointed out. "Do you promise that you will give him his money back? Because if you don't, I will be forced to get my mother involved in this business."

Festus' eyes widened. Then he said sweetly, "Of course, I'll give him his money back, and I apologize for saying he smelled like a sewer."

Turning to Rube I asked, "That good enough for you?"

The raccoon nodded. "Yeah, sure. And I'm sorry I called him a horse's . . . "

I stopped him mid-sentence. "Never mind, we get the idea. So, you two good?"

"Doll," Rube said, "the only way I'm gonna be good is for my paws to touch dirt."

"Okay," I nodded at Lucas, "put him down. Now, if we're done with the peace negotiations, let's go find out what's in that house."

It's a shame that no one was there to film us in slow motion as we approached the porch. The camera effect might have made us look brave and determined. You know, like gunslingers walking out at high noon to face the outlaws?

Truth be told, I don't think any of us really wanted to venture inside. I, for one, dragged my heels going across the overgrown yard.

We stopped at the bottom of the steps. No one said anything until Tori took charge. "Come on people. It's daylight and it's not like we've never dealt with a ghost before. Let's find this thing and talk to it."

"Don't look at me," Rube declared. "I ain't being first again."

"Oh for heaven's sake," I said. "I'll go first."

I made it as far as the front hall. Work with me on the visual here.

Hoarders meets *Practical Magic* with a side of *Storage Wars*.

For those of you who don't watch much TV, we are talking mountains of junk — magical junk. Hazarding a glance over my head, I realized I was standing under a canopy of dried herb bundles.

The others stepped into the space with me. Tori let out a

low whistle. "Just a thought here, Jinksy, but maybe you should be extra careful about what you touch around here."

She didn't have to convince me. Psychometry is my strongest power. I get visions from objects. Until we knew what we were dealing with, I wouldn't be risking filling my mind with unexpected images from anything in this place.

Sometimes what I see becomes entirely too immersive and scary. The house already overwhelmed me without any psychic visions tossed in for flavor.

"What is all this stuff?" Connor asked. "This doesn't look like a normal human household."

"It isn't," Tori said. "This place is filled with things a hoodoo doctor would use."

Over the next few minutes as we wandered through the downstairs rooms, she kept up a running commentary on the contents of the house.

We found baskets of dirt dauber nests.

"You can use the dried mud from the nests to break up relationships or drive off your enemies," Tori explained. "It's also good for workings meant to control people."

Red brick dust for protection.

"It's a centuries old practice going all the way back to Ancient Egypt when red ocher clay had sacred significance."

Bundles of sage for smudging away negative energy.

"Native American influence. You should use the sage with an abalone shell to contain the burning bundle and a feather to disperse the smoke."

In what appeared to be a storeroom, Lucas gingerly opened a glass-fronted cabinet so filthy it was impossible to see what was inside.

"Okay," he said, "I'll bite. What is Goofer Dust?"

"Depends on the conjure," Tori said absently. "The blend is usually proprietary, but Granny Mo made hers with rattlesnake skins and graveyard dirt along with some other stuff."

"And did what with it?"

"Enemy hexes."

Of course. What else would you use Goofer Dust for?

Note that nowhere in these exchanges were any comments made about candles even though the danged things were everywhere. Some were in tall glass jars that looked like the ones Catholics use. Later on, Tori told me those are called blessing candles.

I should have asked about Seven Knob Wishing Candles, which is what I lit when Lucas and I entered the room with the rolltop desk where Rube said he encountered the Petting Ghost.

Yes, yes. I know. We'd already talked about touching things and the risk of accidentally triggering my psychometry. I still can't tell you why I lit the candle that looked like seven squashed meatballs stacked one on top of the other.

You already know about Tori's immediate and outraged reaction, and the way she cross-examined me about my intention in the instant the flame of the match touched the wick.

What I can tell you is that after that, things started getting weird in the house *fast*.

Chapter Twelve

"Miss Glory, I do not think I should leave you alone," Beau said. "You have always expressed considerable apprehension at the prospect. I fear now that you are simply being generous in your assertion that I should attend my meeting."

Glory put her hands on her hips. She was standing in the center of the blotter on Beau's desk beside an open iPad. "Honestly, Colonel." I am a grown woman. I don't need a babysitter. The fairy mound will take care of me, and Chase is right next door if I need anything."

"But how will you occupy your time?"

Throwing her hands up in frustration, Glory said, "For heaven's sake, we are working on a major cataloging project. I have at least 50 newly tagged items to enter into the database. I don't think there's much chance I'll get bored. Now go on. That pretty Miss Linda Albert will be disappointed if you're not there to hear her paper."

At the mention of Linda's name, Beau's face brightened. "She really is a most capable historian, and tonight her subject is of considerable interest to me. It involves the first accusation of witchcraft against a citizen of North Carolina. Miss Linda would not divulge much about her research save that the matter of witch hunting was dealt with quite differently here than in Calvinist New England."

"Go!" Glory said, making a shooing motion with her hands. "Go to the meeting so you can come back and tell me all about it. I'll be waiting on pins and needles to hear what Miss Linda has to say."

"Well," Beau said, his resolve weakening. "If you are sure you will not be offended."

"I will be offended if you *don't* go. Now git! You don't want to be late."

As Beau started for the stairs, Duke the ghost coonhound stood up to follow. "Not this time, boy," the colonel said. "I need you to stay here and look after Miss Glory. Will you do that?"

The dog turned baleful eyes toward his master but solemnly nodded his head. Glory waited until the sound of Beau's boot heels on the wood floor faded upstairs to speak to the dog.

"You're not a snitch, are you Duke? I don't have to hide what I'm getting ready to do from you, do I?"

Cocking his head to one side, Duke whined uncertainly.

"I just mean that no matter what you see, I don't want you to start baying at the moon or attracting anyone's attention, do you understand? This is going to be a secret between us — that is unless it works, and then everyone is going to know."

The dog looked confused, but he nodded anyway.

"Good boy. This is something private I've been planning for ever so along. If what I have in mind goes the way I hope it will then everything — and I do mean absolutely *everything* is going to change for me."

Climbing on her broom, Glory crossed the lair and landed on Tori's alchemy table. She disembarked and stowed the broom against one of the test tube holders, careful not to knock anything over in the process.

"Alright Glory," she said to herself, "just because they all say what you want to do is hard doesn't make it hard. Miss Oprah Winfrey always says that a person has to know their own truth and live it. Well, Glory Green was not destined to live the rest of her life as a green Barbie doll. That is not going to happen. I prayed to the Baby Jesus and Elvis, and I know this is the right thing to do."

She took a rumpled slip of paper out of her pocket and scrutinized the list of ingredients. It had taken her weeks of research alone in the stacks where the others never went to figure out what she needed.

Then it took even more time to watch Tori and take notes on the things that she and Gemma talked about when they worked on their alchemy projects. Both of them were good about labeling the vials and bottles littering the top of the table, but my heavens some of the containers were big!

By the time Glory wrestled everything into position, sweat beaded her brow.

No, scratch that. Ladies do not sweat, they glow.

She was *glowing*, from exertion and from excitement.

Duke, attracted by the motion and the sounds, came over to watch. He wasn't tall enough to see the surface of the table from the floor, so he jumped up on one of the leather sofas and followed her movements with interest.

"This is how a person is supposed to feel when they take back control of their life," Glory told him. "I am glowing because I am empowered. Do you know what that word means, Duke? It means you are the master of your own fate."

At the word "master," Duke's ears went up.

"Not your master, silly," Glory said, shoving a heavy crockery bowl into the center of the table. "He's over at the historical association courting Miss Linda. I looked her up on the Internet. Everybody in town thinks the world of her. She knows everything there is to know about Briar Hollow. Well, except all the stuff she can't know, like about the fairy mound and how she's kinda dating a dead man who isn't really dead because he has a fancy necklace under his shirt. But then if she knew that, she might think the colonel is light in his loafers, and we can't have that, and it really doesn't matter about him being dead because he kind of isn't . . . "

Duke listened intently to the monologue thinking to himself that she never made quite as much sense as the other humans in the lair.

Glory took his attentive presence as interest, so she kept up her running commentary, enumerating the ingredients she struggled to add to the bowl in the proper amounts.

That part of the process didn't go as smoothly as she'd hoped. Some things fell into the mixture with heavy plopping sounds while others poured too quickly for her to control.

When faint smoke circled up from the bowl's interior, Glory regarded it with a combination of stubborn optimism and denial.

"Every cook knows you don't have to follow the recipe *exactly*," she assured Duke. "It's about getting the proportions more or less right. Now all I have to do is mix everything together."

Pushing and shoving, Glory managed to get a book next to the bowl that she used as a platform to reach the top.

Climbing precariously onto the rim, she balanced herself with the handle of a wooden spoon that looked massive in her hands.

"Okey-dokey," she said, "now I'm going to walk in circles like a little human Mixmaster."

The image made Glory giggle as she started around the bowl. She made it halfway before her balance faltered. Panicked, she held onto the spoon for dear life trying desperately to right herself, but then, the spoon slipped, and Glory tumbled head first into the potion.

A beam of green light shot up out of the bowl, striking the ceiling of the lair where it flattened into a roiling mass.

Duke yelped and dove for cover under Beau's desk, peeking out and whining when lurid orange lightning bolts crackled through the green cloud. One long finger of electricity snaked down toward the table where it struck the bowl sending a plume of smoke pouring out of the interior.

That's when the ghostly coonhound covered his eyes with his paws. He didn't want to see what was going to happen next.

A resounding thunderclap shook the lair followed by an ominous silence.

Lifting his head cautiously, Duke's eyes fell on the space in front of the fireplace. His tail began to thump happily against the wooden desk right before he threw his head back and howled.

NEXT DOOR in the cobbler shop Chase felt a vibration move through the building followed by a nauseating wave of power. Duke's unearthly baying split the night air.

Something major must have happened in the fairy mound.

Throwing down his tools, Chase jogged for the back door, breaking into a run when he reached the passageway leading to the lair.

But when he turned the corner, Chase skidded to a stop. There, in front of the fireplace, a willowy, thin woman stood alone staring down at her own body.

As Chase stared, too, he realized something about her seemed familiar.

The black witches robes. The stylish, red high-heels.

"Glory?" Chase asked in a stunned voice. "Is that you?"

The woman nodded numbly. "Am I big?"

"Yes, er, no," he stammered. "I mean you're normal sized"

"And I'm not green?"

The anxious hope in her voice almost broke his heart. "You're not green. You're all pink and flushed, but you're definitely not green. How on earth did you do this?"

Glory met the question with a radiant smile. "I did what Miss Glenda Good Witch said to do."

Chase blinked. "Glenda Good . . . from *The Wizard of Oz?*"

Glory nodded enthusiastically. "When she told Dorothy how to go back to Kansas, although honestly, I don't know *why* Dorothy wanted to go back to Kansas, except maybe because Auntie Em and Uncle Henry needed her, but anyway, that's when Miss Glenda said something that gave me the idea."

Trying to follow her train of thought, Chase said, "I've seen the movie, but you're going to have to help me out here. What did Glenda tell Dorothy?"

"Miss Glenda said, 'You had the power all along, my dear,'" Glory answered earnestly. "I've been thinking about trying this for so long because the others just could not seem to make it happen for me even though they tried — and I do think they did try — but it wasn't a priority for them because they thought I was okay being small. So I started studying on my own, and I just did it, Chase, I made myself big again. And not green."

Laughing, Chase held out his arms to her. "Yes, you did. Congratulations!"

Glory hugged him so hard he thought his ribs would break. "Thank you! Thank you *so much*, Chase. I am *so* happy!"

He thought she was talking about her transformation, but that's not what Glory was talking about at all.

Chapter Thirteen

Myrtle sat quietly beneath the branches of the Mother Tree, eyes closed in meditation. She sensed, more than heard, Moira's approach, silently sliding over on the bench to make room for her friend.

They spent several silent moments joined in mental conversation with the Oak. When both women slowly opened their eyes, they smiled at one another.

"She is in fine form today," Moira said.

"When is she not?"

"Do you miss being with her?"

"At times," the aos si admitted. "There was great peace within her essence, but I was needed here. Shall we join Barnaby?"

Moira sighed. "Yes, but I fear he will be in a mood."

"Still?"

"Constantly," the alchemist said with frustration. "He does not want to attend the Conference of the Realms. Even before Jinx promised Fer Dorich the Agreement would be brought to an end, Barnaby had no desire to assume his diplomatic duties with the Ruling elders."

As they crossed the common and approached the Lord High Mayor's house, Innis, Barnaby's brownie housekeeper came outside, uncharacteristically slamming the door behind her. When she spotted Myrtle and Moira, she dropped a curtsy.

"Fare thee well?" Innis asked.

"I think perhaps we fare better than thee," Myrtle answered. "What has you slamming doors on this fine morning, Innis?"

The lines in the brownie's face deepened. "The Mayor was forced to speak with Elder Isherwood on the mirror this morning. Words were exchanged, and his Lordship has been in a right foul mood since."

"Oh my," Moira said. "What was the substance of the quarrel?"

Innis feigned indignation. "Alchemist, I would *never* spy on the Mayor's conversations."

Moira and Myrtle exchanged an amused look.

"Of course not," Myrtle said soothingly, "but if the men raised their voices, you could hardly be blamed for hearing what they were discussing, now can you?"

"Raised their voices?" Innis scoffed. "That's putting it mildly. The pair of them made so much racket going at it, I thought the mirror would fair split in two. The poor thing was still vibrating when it wheeled itself out of the parlor."

"And the cause of the disagreement was?" Moira prodded.

Innis glanced around and then answered in a low voice. "Creavit delegates to the Conference of the Realms. The Mayor is quite against their inclusion given all the unpleasantness a few years back."

"I assume you mean the Reformation?" Myrtle asked.

When Innis nodded, the aos si said, "You realize that was 432 years ago."

"Aye," Innis said solemnly, "and a fresh wound it is still.

96

Begging your pardon, but I'm off to Madame Kaveh's to fetch coffee for the Mayor since he informed me mine's not fit to drink."

As they watched her march off, radiating disapproval with every step, Moira suggested, "Perhaps we should go to my workshop first and see how Gareth and Dewey are getting along in their labors?"

To her surprise, Myrtle agreed. "I have no more desire to deal with Barnaby's petulance than you, dear friend. Lead the way."

Turning away from the Lord High Mayor's house, the two women walked leisurely through the Shevington square acknowledging the greetings of passersby, but oblivious to their admiring expressions.

In the way of remarkable beings, Moira and Myrtle did not find themselves remarkable in the slightest. Their tall forms moved in fluid unison, Moira's dark head often inclining toward Myrtle's golden presence as she listened closely to the aos si's comments.

Had anyone dared to eavesdrop on their conversation, they would not have found themselves privy to state secrets or philosophical conundrums. The two friends were discussing the entrants in the impending Shevington Rose Cup competition.

Odds makers favored Stan, the resident Sasquatch, and five-year trophy holder, but Myrtle believed Fiona Ryan stood an excellent chance of unseating his hold on the title.

As they neared the workshop, Moira said, "Hester McElroy does not understand the proper application of unicorn manure. Stan has the deft touch of a master with fertilizer."

Before Myrtle could answer, Moira's dwarven assistant, Dewey, came slamming out of the building in a mood reminiscent of the demeanor Innis exhibited moments earlier.

"Oh dear," Moira said. "We seem to be having an epidemic of ill humor."

As Dewey stomped toward them, she said, "Dare I ask?"

The stout dwarf stopped and planted his fists on his hips. "That young fool is nothing but trouble. This scheme of his will bring Irenaeus Chesterfield down on our heads."

Dewey marched past, mumbling, "I'm going to Madam Kaveh's."

Myrtle waited until he'd gone around the corner toward the High Street to release a lilting laugh. "I do hope Madam's coffee is of exceptional strength today and that she has consumed a fair quantity herself."

"Agreed," Moira said. "Shall we go in and discover what young Gareth has planned that Dewey believes will instigate madness and mayhem?"

"By all means. This is turning into a rather entertaining day."

Gareth quickly rose to his feet when they walked into the spacious workshop with its vaulted ceiling and cavernous fireplace. His worktable, situated opposite Moira's own, was littered with an assortment of chess sets.

"Aos si," he said, bowing deeply, "I did not know you would be visiting today or I would have put my work in better order."

"No need, Gareth," Myrtle said. "Disorder is often the sign of great creativity. Master Dewey, however, seems to believe you are taking us all to the brink of catastrophe."

Gareth, who still affected a monk's robes, although he was not a cleric, allowed annoyance to flash across his round face. "If you will excuse me for being blunt, Dewey is especially ill-tempered, even for a dwarf."

"You have not yet seen Dewey in an ill temper," Moira warned. "Difficult as this may be for you to believe, he's been rather sweet of late."

The younger alchemist blanched. "Good heavens. I cannot imagine, nor do I think I wish to."

Myrtle circled the table examining the chess sets. "Your

current work involves forging a link to your former prison, does it not?"

"It does," Gareth said, his face brightening. "As you know, there were many others imprisoned in the Liszt chess set with me, and the board itself possesses sentience. I wish to liberate my fellow inmates and free the board from its dark purpose."

"Intriguing," Myrtle said, "but you must be in possession of the board, is that not true?"

Gareth nodded. "It is, but I have perfected a binding and summoning spell. Would you like a demonstration?"

"We would," Moira said. "Pray proceed."

Removing all of the chess boards except one that was roughly the size of the Liszt set, Gareth took a beaker from its simmering position over a burner. Holding the glass carefully in a pair of tongs, he poured a few drops into a dish and murmured, *"Ruina, et itinerantur."*

On command, the chessmen slid off the edges of the playing surface as the board levitated, flipped over, and settled back on the table. One at a time the pieces rose and moved into their assigned niches in the interior. When they were all in place, the set closed itself with a resounding "thwack" before shooting off the edge of the table. Gareth caught the board before it could strike the ground and looked expectantly at his audience.

"Impressive," Moira said. "Your skills are evolving nicely."

"Thanks to your instruction, and the marvelous alchemical resources at my disposal in Shevington."

"How do you propose to broadcast the spell to the captive board?" Myrtle asked. "We do not know where Chesterfield is currently in residence."

Gareth shook his head. "I don't have an answer for that question, aos si, but when I do, I plan to send for the Liszt board. I cannot allow my fellow prisoners to languish within its confines for eternity."

"A commendable goal," Myrtle said, "but in this, I must agree with Master Dewey. Taking possession of the board will undoubtedly trigger Chesterfield's ire."

Before he thought, Gareth said, "What doesn't?"

Taking in his flushed cheeks and the strident note in his voice, Myrtle said kindly, "You are not yet recovered from your long ordeal, Master Gareth, pray take care that you undertake these actions for the correct reasons."

Gareth looked down at the board still resting in his hands. "He held me over a pit of fire. He told me that if I didn't give him the correct answers, he'd burn me alive. Irenaeus Chesterfield is a petty, angry, vengeful man. Fate sent me a friend in Connor and together we escaped. I must now be a friend to those who are left behind. Do you think I'm wrong?"

"I do not, but like Dewey, I caution you to take care. Please do not set your plan in motion without first speaking to Moira and Barnaby."

Raising earnest eyes to meet hers, he said, "I would never do such a thing without seeking the aid of you all. You have given me a home and sanctuary. I would not wish to lose my place here."

Moira shook her head, and reached for the chess set, gently prying it from Gareth's fingers. She returned the board to the table and rested her hands on the younger alchemist's forearms.

"You cannot lose your place here, Gareth," she said reassuringly. "Shevington is your home now, and you are safe. You must believe that."

Tears filled Gareth's soft brown eyes. "That's what Chesterfield does to those who fall into his hands. He makes them think there is no safe place."

Chapter Fourteen

"Does Jeff know you rented this van?" Gemma asked, steering the vehicle around sharp, winding curves leading up into the mountains north of Briar Hollow.

"He does not. I told him we were going to Cotterville tonight for a book club meeting."

Gemma snorted. "We've used that excuse for years. If we'd read as many books as we claimed to, we'd have doctorates by now."

From the backseat, Brenna said, "You do not belong to a literary society?"

"Oh," Kelly said, "we belong to a book club, but I don't remember the last time we actually met. Saying we were going to a club meeting was like saying we were going to the library in high school."

Brenna considered the statement. "Ah. A cover story for an assignation with the opposite sex. So your book club was a cloak for extramarital affairs."

At the same time, both of the women in the front seat

choked out a strangled, *"No!"* while Gemma swerved so suddenly the van almost went off the road.

Greer burst into laughter. "Brenna, my dear, you will find that women of a certain age born in the 20th century in spite of their youthful experiences in institutions of higher learning, can have rather prim attitudes toward affairs of the heart once they have married."

"Did you just call us old?" Gemma asked, glaring at the baobahn sith in the rear view mirror.

"Not in so many words," Greer replied complacently, "but can you deny a certain Puritanical attitude in middle age that contradicts youthful peccadillos?"

"If 'peccadillos' means what I think it means, no, but we have never used the book club as a cover to cheat on our husbands. We just don't need men all up in our business about everything."

Brenna nodded. "The opposite gender can be inconvenient in that way. Is that why you are no longer married?"

"Not exactly," Gemma said. "Scrap cheated on me with a younger woman."

Brenna made a low sound in her throat that sounded very much like a growl. "What did you do to him?"

"I divorced him."

The sorceress arched her eyebrows. "Without using your magic to seek retribution?"

Gemma shot a sidelong look at Kelly. "See? I told you any other witch would have turned him into a toad. It's not too late for me to do something to him and that little slut of his."

Twisting in her seat, Kelly said to Brenna, "Do not encourage her."

"I am surprised *you* did not encourage her," Brenna said reproachfully. "Being turned into a toad would be the least of any revenge I would visit upon a man who dared to be unfaithful to me."

Kelly appealed to Greer. "You want to help me out here?"

"Hardly. I would have simply killed him — and if you recall, I did offer at the time the infidelity was disclosed."

Groaning, Kelly turned her attention back to the road. "That's enough of that kind of talk. There will be no plots to get back at Scrap no matter how richly he might deserve it." Then, to change the subject, she said brightly, "So, Brenna, you were in a book club?"

Even though there was still a glint of murder in her eye, Brenna followed Kelly's lead and took up the new topic.

"We did not refer to it as a 'club,' but rather a salon. As you know, I spent an unfortunate amount of time in a cave in the Orkneys. When I came to this country in 1773 and found that my grandson was unwilling to have a relationship with me, I had to occupy my time in some way. I sought to be both productive and inconspicuous."

No one commented on that mild version of the tale of Brenna's pursuit of Alexander Skea and his wife, Knasgowa over a period of 87 years before the pair consigned the sorceress to limbo.

Rightly interpreting the uneasy silence, Brenna laughed outright. The rich, throaty sound reverberated in the cab.

"Ladies," she said merrily, "come now. We have forged a friendship despite the misdeeds of my past. There is no need to dance around the subject of my sordid history. If we do, we'll never be able to talk about anything. I was who I was then, and now I am someone else — thanks in large part to your largesse."

"You more than paid for your choices," Gemma said. "So what was this salon you were talking about?"

During her time in the Middle Realm, Brenna had spent a great deal of time expanding her knowledge of the periods of human history she missed during her two imprisonments.

When she escaped from the cave in the Orkneys, she entered a world in the midst of a period called the Enlightenment.

"Thinkers at the time called it simply the Age of Reason," she said. "Here in the United States, the highest manifestation of the ideas and philosophy of the time was your Revolution to emancipate yourself from British Rule."

"You were in the colonies during the Revolution?" Gemma said.

"In the immediate aftermath. I left Scotland for the New World in 1787. From what I have gathered of the way historians treat that period, a great deal is made about the so-called founding 'fathers.' I shudder to think what Dolly and Abigail would have said about that."

"Dolly *Madison* and Abigail *Adams?*" Kelly asked in fascination.

"Yes," Brenna said. "I never met Dolly in person though we corresponded, but I did know Abigail. How she put up with her husband's long absences, I could never fathom. I also exchanged letters with a number of women in Europe at the time including Mary Wollstonecraft. I have recently discovered her daughter went on to write a rather lurid novel about re-animation called *Frankenstein*."

Gemma shook her head. "We've been talking ever since you came to Briar Hollow, but you're still coming up with mind-blowing revelations."

"Well, given my age, there is a lot of ground to cover. Though I did spend many years brokering power in venues dominated by men, I always longed for the company of intelligent, influential women. When possible, I sought such women out. That is how Greer and I came to be acquainted."

Greer cleared her throat. "As I recall, we became acquainted because we were both pursuing the same man to . . ."

"*That*," Brenna said emphatically, "is a tale for another day."

Everyone cracked up at her hasty deflection. "Don't think you're going to get off that light," Gemma said. "You are going to have to tell us that story, but this time you caught a break. We're here."

She turned the van up a narrow mountain road. Straight ahead, a tall, craggy bluff dominated the horizon.

"The cavern lies within that mountain?" Brenna asked.

"Yes," Kelly said. "We'll get as close as we can and then walk up to the base."

Half an hour later, the four women stood in front of a sheer rock face that looked pale and cold in the moonlight.

Kelly scrutinized a printed photo in her hand by the glow of a flashlight. "This is it. See that rock that looks like a triangle? And that one, that could be a rabbit? This is where the GNATS drone went in."

Gemma squinted at the photograph in Kelly's hand in the uneven light. "That doesn't look like a rabbit. A chicken maybe, but not a rabbit."

"Gem," Kelly said sternly. "Focus."

"Sorry, but I'm nervous. I really think we should take more time to plan this caper. The girls just left this morning."

"And we don't know how long they're going to be gone," Kelly said. "We have to do this now. By the time they get back, it will all be over. Jinx will have a minor fit, but she'll agree that taking Seraphina and Ioana to the Ionescus was the right thing to do."

Shuffling the photos, Kelly held another one out. "This is what the drone pilot saw inside the cave."

The image was grainy, but two caskets bound in silver chains were clearly visible in the center of a vast cavern.

Brenna approached the rock face and held her hands in front of her body. Closing her eyes and chanting softly, she produced probing blue tendrils at the end of each finger. Walking back and forth, she stopped when one of the tendrils shot forward and entered a crack in the stone.

"Here. This is the crevice the GNATS drone utilized."

"Can you follow it?" Kelly asked.

"I can try. Place your hands on my shoulders so that you may see what I see."

The women did as they were told, gasping when images of jagged gray walls shot into their thoughts.

"Do not panic," Brenna said. "We are here, in the open air, not trapped in the walls. Breathe deeply and join your powers with mine."

One after the other they closed their eyes. Greer's power awakened first, generating a dull, bloody glow in the ruby ring on her left hand.

"There you are, my old friend," Brenna whispered, her voice sounding far removed from the clearing where they stood. "Grounded, strong, realistic. I have missed the taste of your power, baobhan sith."

Greer's fingers flexed. "You have changed," she said, the burr of her native Scotland thick on her tongue. "Where once your magic burned with anger, you are caring, empathetic, intuitive. Did this happen to you when you passed through the fire and into the Middle Realm?"

"No. the magic you feel is what was meant to be my birthright. It is the power that never awakened amid the poison of my father's cruelty. Kelly, join us."

When Kelly opened the full flood of her power, a yellow aura materialized around her body, bringing a smile to Brenna's lips.

"Your magic is playful," she whispered, "creative and intelligent. Feel how it intertwines and dances with the twin strand of our magic. Has it always been so for you?"

"No," Kelly said, her eyes glowing brightly in the darkness, "only since I was given the Amulet of Caorunn."

"Gemma, my daughter," Brenna breathed. "Do not hold back."

Centering her attention, Gemma grew still, sending a deep orange glow down the line of her arm and into the hand resting on Brenna's shoulder.

"Vital," Brenna murmured, "vigorous. Worthy of the blood of the Sinclairs. We are joined and stronger as four than ever we were as one. Let us proceed."

Chapter Fifteen

Within seconds of Tori chewing me out for lighting that candle, the air in the tiny room stirred, riffling the scattered papers on the desk.

"That," Tori said ominously, "is not good."

"Can any of you see a spirit in here?" I asked.

Everyone shook their heads, including Rodney who was peering out from the collar of my shirt.

Looking around, I saw that we were missing one werecat. "Where's Festus?"

"Here," he answered, pushing past Connor and coming into the crowded space. Cobwebs festooned his ears and drooped from his whiskers.

"Where have you been?" I said. "You look like you stuck your head some place it didn't belong."

"There's a little storage closet under the stairs. Rube got it open, and we had a look around. The guy who lived here was named Sam Clinton, by the way."

"How do you know that?"

"He subscribed to *National Geographic*. Some of the issues go back to the 1890s. We're going to make a fortune with those on eBay."

Leave it to Festus to keep his eye on the profit motive.

Lucas moved over to the desk and scanned the topmost documents. "Same name here. Samuel F. Clinton. Looks like he corresponded with people all over the country about, well, everything. The newest letter seems to be dated May 12, 2014."

"That means he was living in this house for at least 120 years," Connor said. "Did Cezar mention anything about the occupant of the house being Fae?"

"No, he didn't," I said. "All he told us was that Anton let the old man live here. After his death, strange flashes of light started to be seen in the house."

"The Strigoi didn't investigate?" Lucas asked.

"Given their history, the Ionescus have a remarkably live-and-let-live kind of attitude," I said. "They were content to let the ghost have the house until it attracted enough attention to endanger their privacy."

Clearing my throat, I said, in a louder voice, "We don't mean you any harm. If you'll show yourself, we'd like to talk with you."

The air in the room swirled again, this time sending the papers on the desk fluttering to the floor in a cloud of dust.

"That kind of stuff isn't going to work with us," I said sternly. "We deal with ghosts all the time. We're Fae, so materialize and let's talk about this."

No sooner were the words out of my mouth than the whole desk levitated four feet and dropped with a resounding crash. Every candle in the house flared to life before blinking out as an unearthly moan howled through the corridors.

I'm not sure which one of us made it to the door first, but we didn't stop until we were back under the oak tree.

When Tori caught her breath, she said, "Who's for sleeping under the stars tonight?"

Four hands and three paws shot up in the air. Suddenly camping in the great outdoors sounded really, really good to me.

TORI RELENTED on the magical injunction long enough to let me conjure three tents, some chairs, and a barrier spell encircling our campsite.

While Lucas and Connor puzzled over assembling the portable fire pit, I drew Tori off to one side.

"You've been holding out on me about this hoodoo business," I said.

"Not really. You knew Granny Mo was an old mountain woman."

"Not *that kind* of old mountain woman I didn't."

Tori shrugged. "Sorry. It wasn't something any of us talked about. Dad thought hoodoo was nothing but a bunch of backward hillbilly superstition."

"Did he know about his mother's powers?"

"He knew she had 'strange beliefs,' but he never guessed Granny taught Mom about hoodoo. If Granny had been alive she wouldn't have let him treat Mom the way he did when the truth came out about her magic."

"So what happened in there, do you think that had anything to do with all the hoodoo stuff in the house?"

"Honestly, Jinksy, I don't know, but maybe this will tell us." She held up a worn leather notebook. The crinkled edges of the pages showed multiple stains, and the spine bulged from all the odd bits of paper crammed into the volume.

"Where did you get that?"

"It was on the desk. Everything else fell off, but this stayed in place. I figured that couldn't be a coincidence, so I grabbed it on my way out."

Behind us, I heard a loud *whoosh*. Turning we saw that a perfect campfire had roared to life in the fire pit.

"You used magic to light that," Tori said, pointing an accusing finger at Lucas.

"Prove it," he grinned. "Now, what's for supper?"

We dined on delicious beef stew Tori made from freeze-dried food in a combination worthy of any alchemical experiment. Courtesy of the power pack, we capped off the meal with fragrant cups of coffee and the last of the pecan pie from lunch.

Then, sitting around the fire, we examined the leather notebook. At first, I kept my psychometry well controlled. The entries began as a coherent record of a reclusive man's reading and research habits. He devoted pages to working out chess moves, which, in the days before the Internet, he mailed to opponents around the world.

There were diagrams of plants from the surrounding woods with notations regarding their medicinal and metaphysical uses. Many of the clippings referenced folk medicine from a variety of traditions.

The author seemed to take care about what went into the book, going back and augmenting older pages with fresh notes and insights until the sheets became layered with his intricate thought processes.

About mid-way through the volume, however, the lucidity of the entries started to erode. We found simple words crossed out through multiple failed spelling attempts. Then the lists started. Lists for everything.

The order in which he was to dress every day. *"First socks, then shoes."*

How to cook eggs. *"Fried eggs (flat ones) take oil, boiled eggs (round ones) go in water."*

Then we came on the page where he'd written his name twenty times in a row as if trying to commit it to memory.

Dementia can be hidden for a long time in day-to-day actions, buried under excuses and justifications, dismissed as amusing forgetfulness. The evidence we saw on those pages could not be denied.

Cautiously I opened my psychometry, immediately reeling under waves of confusion and fear so intense I reacted as if I'd been struck. Tori, who grounds me during my visions, laid a restraining hand on my arm.

"Shut it down, Jinksy. We don't need your power to understand what was happening to him."

As soon as that part of my mind closed, the night came back into focus. Lucas looked at me with concerned eyes. "I'm fine," I assured him. "For a minute I could feel what he went through as his mind deteriorated. It was horrible."

"Poor old fellow," Connor said sadly. "All alone up here with no one to help him."

Rube, who was sitting beside me, looked at the book lying open on my lap. "If he didn't have nobody, who's Sylvia?"

"What are you talking about?" I asked.

He reached over my arm and pointed. "Is says, 'Sylvia came today, and now everything will be alright.'"

Flipping through the pages, the name "Sylvia" grew increasingly prominent as the record became less a working notebook and more a rambling diary.

"Sylvia helps me remember the things I need to do each day."

"Sylvia helped me solve the chess problem, so Reginald won't think I've gone crazy."

"Sylvia talks to me in the dark of the night."

"Do you suppose someone really did come up here and help him?" Tori ask.

"More to the point," Lucas said. "Was it a someone or a some*thing*?"

"That's what we have to go back in there and find out tomorrow," I said. "We're safe behind the barrier spell. For now, why don't we try to enjoy being up here in the mountains? I mean seriously, have any of you looked up at those stars?"

It never occurred to me that a town as small as Briar Hollow created light pollution, but in the utter blackness of the countryside the twinkling lights overhead glittered like jewels.

With the crackling of the fire and the soothing effects of a hot meal and good company, everyone was more than willing to take my suggestion.

By 9 o'clock Festus and Rube had curled up on opposite ends of the same sleeping bag. Within minutes, their synchronized snoring blended in with the forest sounds. Rodney struggled to keep his eyes open but quickly lost the battle.

Lucas took off his hat and used a towel to make a nest for the rat. Handing the hat to me, I carefully deposited it between Festus and Rube.

The four of us talked long past midnight. I had initially expressed some concern about the fire being visible from the road, but we quickly realized that only the highest dormer on the roof could be seen from the highway below.

Inevitably the topic we decided to avoid came back up again.

"If people see lights up here," Lucas said, staring speculatively at the dark house, "they have to be coming from the attic."

"How do you know it's an attic?" Connor asked, craning his neck back and staring up at the dim outline of the building.

"I don't know for certain," Lucas said, "but it's a good guess when you look at how the house is built. I don't think the space up there is big enough to suggest a third floor."

Then, as if on cue, a light flickered in the attic window. I sat up abruptly from what had been a comfortable position reclining against Lucas' shoulder. Tori and I barely avoided bumping heads when she all but knocked Connor over to bring herself upright.

"You saw that, right?" she said, her eyes still on the window.

"I saw it. Lucas? Connor?"

"Yes," they replied in unison.

Whoever or whatever was in that house seemed to be toying with us, but one thing was already a given — it was most certainly *not* a garden-variety ghost.

Chapter Sixteen

Beau cut through the courthouse lawn, crossing the grass with almost a bounce in his step. He considered with pleasure the aplomb with which Linda presented her paper on the case of *Thomas Bouthier vs. John & Susannah Evans* in 1703.

Bouthier accused Susannah of complicity in the death of his wife, Deborah, by the use of witchcraft. Given his new associations in the 21st century, Beau had devoted a considerable amount of his time to understanding the interaction of mortals and witches in the human realm.

He'd found a sordid record of trumped up charges, ludicrous evidence, unchecked religious fervor, and all too often, death by execution. When Linda invited Beau to attend the presentation and told him about the subject of her paper, he'd been both flattered by her attention and intrigued by the topic.

Neither disappointed him. Linda gave a superb performance and chaired a rousing discussion afterward. The Bouthier case itself proved to have had most unexpected results that still had the colonel bemused as he walked back to the store.

The grand jury, apparently put out that their time was being wasted over such foolishness returned a rather remarkable no bill.

"*Wee of Ye Jury find no bill,*" Linda read from her notes, "*and ye person IGNORAMOUS and it is Ordrd that the sad Sussnh Evens be acquitted pay the charges.*"

Linda then showed a slide with an image of the original document to illustrate that the word "ignoramus," rendered in the spelling of the day, had been set down in all capital letters.

Armed with this new and thoroughly delightful information, Beau looked forward to cross referencing the account with Fae histories of the period to discover how actual witches reacted to the verdict.

A motion to his left caught the colonel's attention. There, in one of the lower courthouse windows, the ghost of Howard McAlpin, or at least the right half of him, was making a rather rude gesture in Beau's direction.

But not even the surly former mayor could ruin the colonel's good mood. In response, Beau swept off his Panama hat, bowed low to His Honor, and resumed his walk.

Out of the corner of his eye, he saw McAlpin's apparition waver and crumble. "Poor fellow," Beau mumbled, "he simply cannot understand that to maintain a coherent manifestation, one must focus."

Using his key, Beau let himself in the front door of the Witch's Brew. The building felt empty without Jinx and Tori in residence. Hopefully, he would find Greer and Brenna in the lair, returned from their mysterious errand in the company of Kelly and Gemma.

Instead, when he opened the basement door and stepped through the invisible barrier that separated the fairy mound from the human realm, Beau encountered a solid wall of sound.

In the many months Glory had lived with them, the colonel

had become familiar with the voice of Elvis Presley. Glory seemed to have an endless capacity to listen to the unfortunate young man's music for hours at a time.

The current composition, a raucous tune called "Jailhouse Rock" was, if Beau had cared to admit it, one of his favorites.

But instead of seeing the little witch dancing alone on the top of his desk, her habit when she took a break from cataloging artifacts, the colonel's eyes met a most remarkable sight.

There, in the middle of the lair, Chase McGregor danced a vigorous jitterbug with a lovely young woman. Like the others, Beau knew Jinx had made her decision to give her affections to Lucas Grayson, so he was surprised to find Chase in the company of another female so quickly.

The couple caught sight of him standing on the stairs. Then, in a move that took him considerably aback, the woman rushed forward with a cry of, "Colonel Longworth! Look at me! I'm big again!"

She hit him full force, throwing her arms around him in a crushing hug.

"Forgive me, madam," Beau stammered. "Are we acquainted?"

Pulling back, she regarded him with an expression of elation. "Beau, you silly thing! It's me. Glory!"

He studied her face intently before recognition dawned. "Miss Glory! It *is* you! How has this miraculous turn of events come to pass?"

"Well," she said, ducking her head, "I did some research and tonight when I was all by myself, I decided to try it out, and this is what happened."

She emphasized the word "this" with a twirl that sent her black robes flaring around her. "You're just in time. I have some of the goop left, and I'm going to try to make my stuff bigger, too. You can watch!"

Beau looked over at Chase, who shut off the music. "Were you here when this occurred?"

"No, I was next door working and I heard the explosion."

The colonel's eyebrows shot up. "Explosion? Is that going to happen again?"

"I don't think so," Glory said, tripping down the stairs and retrieving Graceland East from the shelf over Beau's desk. "That was because I fell into the mixing bowl, which wasn't part of the original plan."

While the men watched, she lifted the front away from the dollhouse. Using her index finger, she sorted through the clothes in her closet and pulled out a stylish red dress with a contrasting white collar.

"Now this one," she said, "will go with my shoes."

She carefully laid the dress on the conference table, rummaged around among Tori's supplies, and came up with an eyedropper, which she dipped in the bowl.

The implement came out filled with a shimmering, iridescent liquid. "Okay," she said, holding the dropper over the dress. "You all stand back now in case I get any on the table."

Beau and Chase exchanged an uneasy look as they both moved several steps farther away.

Glory squeezed the black bulb and held her breath as a single drop fell on the garment. With a resounding "*pop*," the dress expanded to normal size.

Squealing happily, Glory snatched up the dress. "If you all will excuse me, I need to change!"

She ducked into one of the guest rooms the fairy mound created during the Freak Freeze and closed the door behind her.

"My heavens," Beau said, "I have never seen her so infectiously happy."

"Wouldn't you be if you'd been living as a miniature green witch all this time?" Chase asked, settling in one of the chairs in front of the fireplace. "You might as well sit down, Beau. If I know women as well as I think I do, she's not going to stop at enlarging one dress. Then she'll want to try every one of them on. We, my friend, are in for a style show."

Beau took the chair opposite Chase. "This is a ritual with which I am familiar. When my wife's dress maker came for the final fitting of her gowns, I was required to play witness and venture my opinion."

"How'd that go?"

"Cautiously. I found that if I watched Almira's face closely, I could ascertain and thus mirror her feelings about a particular gown."

"Smart man. When I . . . "

He never finished the sentence. Glory stepped out of the guest room wearing the red dress, which showed off a pair of shapely legs tapering down to the high-heeled Louboutins that were her prized possession.

"How do I look?" she asked, running her hands through her shoulder length, reddish brown hair and pulling it back. "Should I wear my hair up or down?"

Taking the diplomatic route, Beau said, "I find you equally lovely with either coiffure."

Glory turned to Chase. "What do you think?"

Blinking a couple of times before he answered, Chase stammered, "I like it up."

That won him a dazzling smile. "I think so, too. Now, I like this dress, but I have a purple pantsuit that's so much fun. I'm going to make that one big next."

As she busied herself with the transformation, Beau leaned toward Chase and said, "You surmised correctly in regard to the impending style show."

"Huh?" Chase said, his eyes still on Glory.

"I said you are correct that she will enlarge and try on multiple items of clothing."

"Oh, yeah, right," Chase said absently. "Has her hair always been that color?"

Beau frowned. "So long as I have known her, yes. Why?"

"Be back in a flash!" Glory said, snatching up the now normal-sized pant- suit and heading back into her impromptu changing room.

"I just never noticed how pretty she is."

Reaching into the breast pocket of his coat, Beau took out a pipe and lit the tobacco. "Ascertaining her visage was more difficult when she was green." I find her complexion much more pleasing now, wouldn't you agree?"

"I would," Chase said thoughtfully. "I sure would."

Chapter Seventeen

B renna's magic probed the cracks and crevices in the stone, following the faint energy signature left by the GNATS drone. At last, she reached an opening, so infinitesimal not even the minuscule craft had been able to proceed.

With their powers intertwined, Kelly, Gemma, and Greer had followed Brenna's tortuous progress through the mountainside. At the seemingly dead end, Greer said, "What do you propose we do now?"

"Unlike the drone, physical size does not constrain our efforts," Brenna replied. "Remain calm. Before our shared awareness enters the cavern, you will experience an instant of intense claustrophobia. Ready?"

"As ready as we're ever going to be," Kelly said. "Do it."

In the second required to negotiate the opening, their perception of the world choked, drawing a gasp from Gemma's lips and sending a tremor through Kelly's body. Only Greer remained silent and calm as utter blackness descended.

"Do not panic," Brenna counseled. "Work with me to send illumination into the darkness."

A pinprick of light appeared that grew slowly until the details of the space became visible — abandoned cabinets, a pair of tall chairs, a cold fire pit, and in the shadows beyond, two caskets bound with silver chains.

"There they are," Kelly said. "Can we get closer?"

"The thread of our magic grows thin," Brenna said. "It may snap at any moment. Be prepared."

As they inched forward, static destroyed the clarity of the image, forcing Brenna to bring their motion to a crawl. Her breathing grew rough and labored from the effort until finally, they hovered over the caskets on a gossamer filament of power.

"My next action will most likely destroy our connection to the interior," Brenna said, "but it may give us additional information."

"What are you going to do?" Gemma asked.

"I am going to touch one of the caskets."

"*No!*" Greer said, her voice low and urgent. "You must not attempt to touch the mind of a vampire so imprisoned."

But the warning came too late.

Boundless hunger sliced through them punctuated by undulating howls. Gemma fell to her knees, dragging Kelly down with her. Greer stayed on her feet, but green flames filled her eyes as she backed away from the others.

Brenna reached for her in concern, but Greer held up her hand. "Do not approach me," she whispered hoarsely. "I feel their hunger for blood. Give me a moment."

Gemma recovered first, rising unsteadily and helping Kelly to her feet. "That's what they're experiencing in those boxes?" Kelly asked in horror. "Brenna, there's no question now. We have to get them out of there. Can we do it?"

"I believe we can," Brenna said, "but it must be now, while the impressions of the interior are fresh in our minds. Are you up to the task?"

"We have to be," Kelly said firmly. "I'll never sleep another night if we leave Seraphina and Ioana in there now. What do you need from us?"

"First, we must cast a circle," Brenna said. "Remove everything from this clearing. All the loose rocks, branches, and leaves. Cleanse the area as thoroughly as possible."

When they were done, Brenna took a small sack of salt out of her backpack. "Once the circle is cast, no matter what occurs, we cannot leave this space. Gemma, did you bring the candles?"

Opening her own pack, Gemma took out four candles: green, yellow, blue, and red.

"Excellent," Brenna said. "Place the candles in each of the corresponding cardinal directions in an area wide enough to contain us and the two caskets."

Gemma paced off the space, setting out the four candles as directed before rejoining her companions in the center of the clearing.

As they watched, Brenna traced the periphery of a circle from one candle to the next, lighting the wicks, and leaving a trail of salt in her wake. With the flaring of each flame, Brenna blessed the creatures and spirits of the North, South, East, and West in turn.

Next, she retraced her steps three times. "Thrice I conjure thee, Circle of Power," she intoned. "Repel the spirits of evil and shield us from their wickedness. Contain and preserve the power we raise within."

As the last words fell from her lips, light shot up from the salt crystals, encasing the women behind a shining barrier.

Brenna drew a small dagger from her pack and looked at Greer. "To accomplish this summoning, I must use the powers of necromancy, spilling my blood into the periphery of the circle. Is your hunger in check?"

"It is. The circle you have cast contains my darkness as effectively as that of the Strigoi you seek to liberate."

The sorceress smiled. "You are not dark, old friend. If you were, this circle would have done far more than contain you."

Greer returned the smile. "You did not bother to mention that."

"I did not need to. I knew you would not be harmed."

"Can you say the same for Seraphina and Ioana?" Kelly asked.

"If I am successful," Brenna said, "their caskets will come with them. If I am not, we will have something of a problem with which to contend."

"Meaning?" Gemma asked.

Greer supplied the answer. "If the girls appear unbound, we cannot risk opening the circle without setting them free. We will be trapped along with them inside the confines of this space."

Gemma threw a reproachful look toward Brenna. "That's another significant detail you failed to mention."

"We will deal with that situation should it arise," Brenna said crisply, "for now, our concentration should be focused on preventing that need to develop at all."

"Agreed," Kelly said. "Let's get on with it."

Using the tip of the dagger, Brenna cut her left palm, curling her fingers into a fist as blood welled from the open wound. Walking the circle a fourth time, she allowed the crimson drops to fall onto the salt.

The shining barrier flared, shutting out the night sounds of the forest. Now encased in a space of unnatural stillness, Brenna held out her right hand to Kelly and her left to Gemma.

Hesitating, Gemma said, "Shouldn't you bind that cut?"

Spreading her fingers, Brenna displayed her palm, now healed. "Have faith in our magic, daughter. We are not in a space where the rules of humankind apply."

When Gemma took Brenna's hand, Greer stepped forward and completed the circle.

"Join with me in your essence," Brenna said, "as you did when we traversed the mountain."

From within the communion of their magic, Brenna raised her eyes to the moon. "Shadows of Oblivion, I call to thee to surrender thy charges. Bring to me the imprisoned *Strigoi mort blasfematoare.*"

Overhead, in a clear sky, lightning crackled, and the moon grew dark. The howling that had filled their minds in the cavern now entered the circle, born along on a hot, liquid wind.

"Do not drop your hands!" Brenna shouted over the tumult. "We must remain united!"

A second bolt crashed overhead, this time pivoting in the sky and striking the clearing. The metallic scent of blood filled the circle as the faint outline of the two caskets flickered in and out of focus on either side of the witches.

"Concentrate!" Brenna cried. "Will the manifestation to solidify."

She began to chant softly in Latin, joined first by Greer, and then by the others. As their voices gained strength, the lines of the coffins grew sharper until a third bolt of lightning erupted, this time upward from the circle and back into the clouds.

The wind died as suddenly as it arose, and the smell of blood disappeared. The shining wall of the circle dimmed to a faint mist; in the distance, the forest sounds returned.

"Did it work?" Kelly asked weakly.

"It did," Brenna said, squeezing and then releasing her hand. "Look."

There, on either side of them, sat the intact, chained caskets.

"Well, okay then," Gemma said. "We dodged that proverbial bullet. Now, let's take this circle down and see if my solution to moving these crates works."

In response, Brenna walked the circle three times again in a counterclockwise path, thanking the spirits of the cardinal directions as she progressed. On the last transit, she declared the circle closed. The last of the shimmering barrier fell away.

As they dispersed the salt with branches standing in for brooms, Kelly said, "Brenna, you opened and closed the quarters in a way I haven't heard before."

"My magic is old," Brenna replied. "I learned to cast a circle centuries ago. I know no other way."

"We should start taking notes on how your magical workings differ from what we were taught," Gemma said thoughtfully. "You're like a living encyclopedia of magical evolution."

"It would please me to study with you both, but for now, I believe we must set academic considerations aside, unless you want to risk being caught by humans with two chained caskets in our possession when the sun rises."

"Good point," Gemma said. "I don't even think I could come up with an explanation for that one, and I'm famous for my concocted stories."

Digging in her pack again, she removed a corked flask. "If the weight calculation is correct, this levitation potion should suspend the caskets long enough for us to get them down to the van."

Unstopping the bottle, she poured a thin line down the middle of the first casket. The liquid expanded when it touched the surface, creating an opaque film over the polished wood.

"*Supernatet.*"

With barely a wobble, the casket rose to waist level and floated serenely in the air.

"*Yes!*" Gemma said, pumping her fist. "Score one for the alchemist!"

She repeated the application and spell on the second casket with identical results.

"We are good to go," Gemma said, taking hold of one of the handles on the nearest coffin and motioning to Kelly to do the same.

With only a flicker of reluctance, Kelly complied. The two women stepped forward, steering the heavy box as if it weighed no more than a feather. Brenna and Greer took control of the other casket, and the strange procession descended toward the waiting van.

Later, when Kelly told the story to Jinx, she would recall what she thought at that moment. "*This turned out to be easier than I expected.*"

"Huge mistake."

To which her daughter would reply, "Join the club."

Chapter Eighteen

She watched as the beings climbed to the house from the field below. They made for a strange assembly — four humans, a mountain lion, a raccoon, and a rat. Or so she thought.

As the group moved within the field of her senses, she felt their Fae blood and recoiled with caution. No creatures from the Otherworld had ever come to this place.

That explained to her, in part, Sam's great loneliness. He told her that he must forever be separated from his kind to fulfill the mission entrusted to him.

Since Sam's passage into the fabric of the Universe, only the Strigoi and the three young humans seeking spirits had crossed the boundary of this land.

When they came, she had wished to leave with them, to explore the world beyond the crumbling dwelling, but Sam's magic bound her. Until another practitioner undid his workings, she could not leave.

She.

Sam had called her "Sylvia."

A garbled play on her true identity born of the twisted wreckage of his mind.

In time, she came to think of herself as Sylvia, taking into her heart and making her own the name that recalled for her decades of companionship with the complicated, confused old man.

When the Fae reached the overgrown yard, they set to tearing away the thick vines guarding the entrance. The boldness of their incursion worried her. Coming, as they did, with no invitation or summons, was their intent liberation or destruction?

The raccoon, in the way of his kind, broke from the others and took independent action. Wriggling his body through the plants, he reached the door ahead of the others, scampering into the deserted hallway, which he appraised with black, glittering eyes.

It amused Sylvia to listen to his running commentary of self-dialogue. Sam spent hours talking to himself, taking both parts of the conversation, winning and losing arguments with himself according to rules only he comprehended.

She did not, however, appreciate hearing the words "junk" and "crap" in reference to Sam's possessions. The clutter in the house reflected the disarray of his thoughts. It was visible evidence of a condition to be pitied, not judged in an avaricious search for valuables.

Sylvia felt a surge of annoyance. Was this raccoon both an invader *and* a common thief? She followed his waddling progress down the side hall and into Sam's office where he scaled the chair and rifled through Sam's notes.

In spite of herself, Sylvia became fascinated with the raccoon's black paws, which he used as dexterously as humans used their hands. Sometimes she longed for a more corporeal form if only to experience creativity and accomplishment as something more than abstracts.

Extending herself delicately, Sylvia tried to feel the enticing silver fur on the raccoon's front leg. At the suggestion of pressure on its body, the animal froze, watching in something akin to horror, as the hairs lay flat under her gentle probing.

Then, to Sylvia's shock and surprise, he shot up from the chair and made a mad dash for the front door. The flight left her chagrined. She had meant no harm by her curiosity.

She could not, however, give in to her desire to communicate — to apologize for the fright she had caused. The cloak of her natural invisibility afforded her refuge and stability. Sylvia dared not betray her presence until she understood why the Fae were here and ascertained what they wanted.

The way into the house now lay open, but the Fae appeared occupied in resolving a dispute between the raccoon and the mountain lion. The cat, she noted, appeared to be aged and limped heavily on one hind leg, but that did not diminish his apparent vitality.

After some period of negotiation, the group reached an accord and approached the house. As they neared, Sylvia remembered what Sam used to mutter as he peered through the glass on either side of the door.

"The forest has eyes. The woods have ears. I will see. I will be silent. I will hear."

She asked him once about the words. "An old proverb," he replied. "Old and wise. Be silent when you would think to speak, Sylvia. Hear when others do not know you listen."

Heeding the admonition, she rose halfway up the stairs, hovering in the shadows and waiting.

Once inside, the group stood in the hallway discussing Sam's possessions. At this proximity, she realized the taller of the two women was a witch. Her magic called to Sylvia with the breath of a cleansing wind.

The man with the hat smelled like an elf, but damp. There was much water in his soul. Earth forged the essence of the second male. His scent was that of animals and growing things. The smaller woman carried within her the spark of fire.

Air. Water. Earth. Fire.

Sylvia could see the elemental threads weaving the four of them into an ever-deepening tapestry with each passing second.

As for the others, the mountain lion was a shifter; the raccoon a traveler of the realms. But the rat? The rat confused her. She could not fathom his true nature and stirred uneasily when he stared too long in her direction. That one knew far more than he cared to let on.

She followed the group through the house, hanging back, so they did not feel the air stirring. What she would come to think of as the Remarkable Thing, happened in the office. The witch lit a candle.

A wishing candle.

When the flame in her hand brought the wick to life, the intention in her heart was strong.

"I want to find you so we can go home."

We. Home.

There it was. The invitation for which Sylvia had longed. The words that brought her exile to an end. The witch sought to free her from this lonely place and take her to a new home!

In her excitement, Sylvia swirled the air in the room by mistake, an action the Fae wrongly interpreted as potentially harmful. When Sam allowed her to escape the Middle Realm on that long ago night, their first encounter had been different.

But Sam was different.

He used his magic to "travel" without ever leaving the house. He opened windows on the realms, watching events, seeing fantastical sites. Building his understanding. Sylvia joined him in his pursuits, overjoyed to be free once again to explore and content with her companion.

But now Sam was gone and she had not yet found a way to make these Fae understand.

As the raccoon had done earlier, everyone in the group seemed to fixate on the desk. Was that a way to make them see?

Summoning all her strength, Sylvia moved into the space under the desk and raised it from the floor before flowing out again to gauge the reaction she caused.

To her disappointment, all of them, including her new friend the witch, ran for the front door. But why would the sorceress call to her with her magic if she did not know Sylvia was there?

At the door, Sylvia watched as the Fae retreated to the old oak at the edge of the lawn. There, the witch conjured shelter for the group and, inexplicably, cast an energy barrier.

Sylvia hovered long at the front entrance, watching as the group built a fire, consumed their evening meal, and examined Sam's notebook. The smaller woman had taken the book from the office at the moment the others began their wild flight to the outside.

When Sylvia was sure the Fae had fallen asleep, she moved down the steps and across the lawn, a mere whisper against the grass. Outside the barrier of magic, she looked longingly at the sleeping witch.

The others called her "Jinx." She seemed both powerful and kind. Sylvia longed to know her. To share with the witch the story of her years with Sam and of the time before that in the Middle Realm after the Great Segregation.

A movement low on the ground caught Sylvia's attention. The rat, who had been sleeping curled in the elf's hat, crossed the grass to stand opposite her on the other side of the barrier.

Curious, Sylvia whispered on the night wind, "Can you see me, Little Brother?"

The rat stood up on his hind legs and used his front paws to draw a hazy outline, squinting his eyes and cocking his head to one side.

"You can, but not well. I do not know how this is possible, but I welcome your recognition."

The rat ran over to Sam's notebook, which lay open on the grass beside the sleeping witch. Placing one paw on the page, he placed the other over his heart and hung his head.

"Thank you. I do grieve for him, My Brother, but for him, the way here was no longer clear. Only by going into the Universe could he hope to know clarity once more."

Joining her again, the rat pointed toward the house, as the light flashed in the attic, and then gestured toward Sylvia in question.

"No. I do not cause the light, I guard it in Sam's absence. It must not fall into the hands of any save she who has the heart to receive it."

Joy filled the rat's face. He pointed to the sleeping witch and used his paws to draw a heart in the air, and then a larger one, and a larger one still until his arms could reach no farther.

"You believe her heart is equal to the task?"

The rat's head bobbed up and down emphatically.

"Did they see the light?"

He nodded.

"And tomorrow they will seek it out?"

Another nod.

"Then tomorrow we shall see if the light allows itself to be found. The witch has already summoned me, but regardless, where the light goes, so go I."

The rat sat down and looked at her patiently.

"You wish to hear my story? It is rather long."

When the rat patted the grass, she flowed down to his level, regarding him thoughtfully through the magical barrier. "You are a most unlikely friend, Sir Rat, but I will tell you my tale. It begins with my exile to a place you may know as the In Between . . . "

Chapter Nineteen

Once the caskets were safely stowed in the back of the van under a heavy tarp, the women climbed into the cab and started for the Ionescu compound.

"You do realize it's going to be kind of awkward rolling up on a gated Strigoi community at 1 o'clock in the morning," Gemma said, as she backed the vehicle out of the trees and turned down the dirt road. "Shouldn't we call ahead or something?"

Greer laughed. "The Ionescus will know of our approach long before we reach the gate. The Strigoi sleep little and are, by nature and circumstance, vigilant and watchful."

"Will they also know we have the girls in the back?" Kelly asked.

The baobhan sith shook her head. "No. The silver chains will prevent the Strigoi from detecting Seraphina and Ioana, but Cezar will need to do little more than lay his hand on one of the caskets to know the truth of who lies inside."

Kelly shuddered. "When he senses what we did he won't be able to put them out of their misery soon enough."

"Agreed," Greer said. "The fate they suffer is one any of our kind would do much to avoid."

Kelly started to ask a question, but caught herself, much to Greer's amusement.

"No," the baobhan sith said, "I have never napped in a casket but were I to be confined in the same manner, I would suffer as the Strigoi have suffered."

"That's horrible," Kelly said. "I can't imagine."

Staring out the window, Brenna said in a tight voice, "That is exactly why Irenaeus imprisoned them as he did — because it's unimaginable. I have no doubt the thought of them suffering in the darkness has given that vile man enormous satisfaction."

They rode in silence until Gemma reached the main road and steered the van onto the pavement.

Brenna turned her gaze away from the window and said, "If I may ask, how did a Strigoi community come to settle in the mountains of North Carolina?"

"That," Gemma said, glancing over her shoulder at the sorceress in the backseat, "is actually an interesting story that dates to the American Revolution. I'm surprised you weren't aware of their presence when you were in the area . . ."

Kelly gasped sharply, interrupting the narrative. "Gemma! Look out!"

Jerking her attention back to the road, Gemma saw a white doe standing frozen in the headlights. She slammed on the brakes, but there was no room. The only way to avoid hitting the animal was to swerve.

"Hold on!" Gemma yelled, twisting the wheel and fighting to retain control of the machine.

The doe never moved as the van careened into the forest, bouncing off rocks and trees as it plowed forward.

Even though Gemma was a good driver, the strength of the momentum coupled with the van's center of gravity flipped the vehicle twice before it jarred to a stop, upright but crumpled.

After several seconds, Gemma raised her head, wincing when the muscles in her neck protested the motion. Blinking to clear her vision, she reached for the passenger seat, meeting her friend's probing hand halfway through the space separating them.

"Kelly?" she said hoarsely.

"I'm fine. You?"

"Okay, a little shook up. Brenna?"

"Intact," the sorceress replied. "Where is Greer?"

Struggling to release her seatbelt, Gemma turned to discover the seat behind her empty. "Was she thrown out when we flipped?"

Beside her, Kelly's said quietly. "I don't think *she* was, but they were."

The baobhan sith stood beside the van blocking the advance of two skeletal wraiths — Seraphina and Ioana.

Brenna tried to get out, but her door refused to budge. Swearing, she shoved against the twisted metal with the force of her magic sending the door flying off its hinges.

"Stay in the van," she ordered, as she went to join Greer.

"Not bloody likely," Kelly said, forcing her own door open.

"Right behind you," Gemma said, sliding across the seat and following Kelly outside.

The three women came around opposite ends of the van and moved to stand beside Greer. That's when they saw the baobhan sith's left arm and shoulder hanging at a twisted, distorted angle.

"You were planning to confront them alone with a dislocated shoulder?" Brenna asked conversationally.

"Makes for a fairer fight," Greer said, her voice tight.

Brenna raised her hands to heal the wound, but Greer stopped her. "Later. We have to deal with them now."

Seraphina threw her head back and cackled insanely. "Deal with us? Don't you mean feed us? How fitting, Kelly Ryan, that you should be the first meal of our resurrection."

"If you think you're big enough to take that bite, Seraphina, bring it," Kelly said levelly, raising her hands in preparation. Bright yellow bolts crackled between her fingers.

The Strigoi, who had moved forward stopped. "My, my, *my*," she said, her glassy eyes growing larger in her emaciated face. "You've grown up while we slept."

"You have no idea."

Ioana clutched at her sister's arm. "I'm not going back in that casket," she wailed. "Please, sister. Let's just run."

"That's not an option available to you," Brenna said.

From the road behind them, a car door slammed. "Hey!" a man's voice called. "You all right down there?"

"We're fine," Gemma yelled back. "Already called a tow truck, but thanks for stopping."

"I'll stay here and keep my headlights on so the wrecker can find you," he yelled back. "I've got a First Aid kit. I'll be right there."

Seraphina raised her head and sniffed the night air. "He smells delicious. Perhaps we'll start with him so you can watch."

"Not happening," Gemma barked.

"Oh?" Seraphina asked with feverish, mad eyes. "How are you going to stop us? By killing us in front of him? By showing your magic to a human? By clouding his mind afterward? And the mind of the tow truck driver? And the police? And anyone else who shows up? Shouldn't you be thinking about getting rid of those caskets first, or do normal humans drive around at night with corpses? I forget."

When Gemma hesitated, the Strigoi seized the advantage.

"Let us go," she urged hoarsely. "We have no quarrel with you. Our real fight is with Irenaeus Chesterfield."

Brenna regarded her thoughtfully. "The enemy of my enemy is my friend."

Seraphina turned toward her. "You're new," she said brightly. "Are you a good witch or a bad witch?"

"Bad," Brenna purred, "very, very bad."

"But you see my point, don't you Bad Witch?"

Behind them they heard the motorist moving through the brush toward the wrecked van.

"Kelly," Brenna said, "please attend to the caskets."

Gesturing toward the broken coffins, Kelly murmured, "*Mixtio.*"

The boxes instantly blended with their surroundings. "That will work as long as it's dark," she said. "We'll need a better solution when the sun comes up. It's time to make a decision ladies."

Brenna, her eyes still on the Strigoi, said, "I know it's a deal with the devil, but I think we have to do it."

"Agreed," Kelly said tightly, looking at Seraphina with a mixture of loathing and pity. "You can go, but I'm warning you. Find an alternate food source. If you kill a human, we'll have every Ionescu in North Carolina out looking for you and you know what will happen then."

"We do," Seraphina said. "We seek only the wizard Chesterfield."

As the Strigoi slipped into the night, Brenna held her hands over Greer's shoulder, the palms glowing with healing light. The baobhan sith winced as the joint slid in place, flexing her fingers to test the function of the limb.

"Thank you, and just in time."

A man stumbled around the back of the van with a First Aid kit in his hand. "Sorry it took me so long to get here," he puffed. "I really gotta exercise more. Man! I can't believe you ladies are all right. I was up at the top of the hill and saw you go off the road. That crazy white deer just stood there and watched. Creepy as hell."

While Gemma and Greer kept their would-be Good Samaritan occupied, Brenna and Kelly moved into the shadows at the front of the van.

"I am sorry a better solution did not present itself," Brenna said.

"Don't be silly," Kelly said. "The Strigoi had us over a barrel and they knew it. There was too much happening at one time to contain the situation. What do you think they'll do now?"

"They will have to find a way to feed, most likely on some unfortunate creature in the woods. Once their blood hunger is under control, they will use their wiles to establish themselves somewhere. They were not lying when they said they only seek Irenaeus."

"How do you know?"

"I am gifted with sight. Their auras betrayed their ravenous hunger, but not the telltale spikes of falsehood. For the time being, they will honor the pact they made with us tonight. We have some time to come up with an alternate plan to dispose of them."

Gemma walked up in time to hear the last words. "Jim Ed, our savior over there, is thoroughly smitten with Greer."

"As, no doubt, Greer intends him to be," Brenna said. "She is quite gifted in that fashion."

"Exactly," Gemma replied. "She's doing the full vampire glamor *thing*. When she's done, he'll tell exactly the story we want him to tell. I did have to call Sheriff Johnson. He's on his way. I'll need an accident report for the rental company."

Kelly groaned. "Oh, damn. I put the van on Jeff's credit card. He is gonna have a *fit*."

"About the van or the Strigoi?" Gemma asked.

"The Strigoi could get us killed, but the rental company

could hit his pocket book," Kelly said miserably. "Do you think it's unethical for a wife to use a cooperation spell on her husband?"

"Absolutely not," Brenna said, "especially in the interest of your peace of mind."

"Agreed," Gemma said, "but I don't think that's going to work on the first man we have to talk to."

"Who's that?" Kelly asked.

"Cezar Ionescu."

Chapter Twenty

R odney, of all people, woke me up the next morning.
Okay, of all "rodents." Work with me here.
The point is that I felt something on my chest
and when I peeled open one eye, there he sat on his haunches,
snowy chest shining in the pale morning light. Raising a pink
paw, he waved at me and grinned.

"What the heck time is it anyway?" I asked blearily.

From the sleeping bag on the other side of the tent, Tori
answered in a muffled tone. "Too damn early o'clock."

"Tell that to the rat sitting on my chest."

The smell of coffee hit my nose, triggering a coherent
synapse in my befuddled brain.

"The guys are awake already?" I asked Rodney who
nodded.

That explained my rodential alarm clock.

"Did they send you in here to get us up?"

More nodding.

"Because they knew I wouldn't yell at you?"

That elicited a shrug and an expression in Rodney's bright
eyes that clearly said, "Well, duh."

There was no way I couldn't cave to an appeal that adorable. "Okay, fine. Go tell them we'll be right out."

The Tori-sized lump across from me said, "What's this 'we' stuff?"

Which would be when the scent of bacon and eggs hit her nose.

She came up out of the sleeping bag like a bird dog going on point. "Are they cooking breakfast out there?"

"Smells like it to me."

She started rummaging for her jeans. "Well, come on, Jinksy. Let's get a move-on already."

The fastest way to Tori's enthusiasm is via her stomach.

When we emerged from the tent, Lucas was waiting for me, tin cup in hand. "Good morning," he said, holding out the steaming liquid. "I understand you're not worth shooting until you have your coffee."

"Let me guess," I replied, accepting the cup and a kiss. "You've been talking to Festus."

From the vicinity of the campfire, the werecat said, "Not my fault if I'm the only one around here who'll tell the truth."

Glancing over, I spotted him, still in mountain lion form, licking a plate clean next to Rube who was munching on a biscuit covered in honey. The raccoon waved a sticky paw in my direction and mumbled, with his mouth full, "Morning, Doll."

"You've got honey on your whiskers," I said, trying not to laugh as he went into a frenzy of face licking.

Say what you will about raccoons; they get high marks in my book for personal hygiene.

Tori emerged from the tent running a hand through her blonde spikes. Connor's face lit up at the sight of her. As he rushed to offer her a cup of coffee.

Camping or not, we were getting pretty good room service on this excursion.

As Tori and I settled in to eat our first breakfast, Lucas and Connor started on their second. Tori bit into a thick, flaky, buttered biscuit and sighed with pleasure.

"You cheated like a big dog and used magic to make these and I love you for it," she said.

Lucas grinned and offered her another biscuit. "After what we went through in the house yesterday, I didn't think freeze-dried eggs and self-heating oatmeal was going to cut it."

"Amen," I agreed, shoveling a forkful of hashbrowns in my mouth. "I'm not going back in there with nothing but fake food in my stomach."

Festus pushed his plate aside and began to groom his whiskers. "So what's the plan? Are we just going to waltz back in and let more furniture attack us?"

"No," I said, "we're going straight to the attic, bypassing all belligerent furniture, and locating that mystery light."

To my surprise, Rodney scaled my pants leg, perched on my knee, and pushed against my plate with his paws. The message was clear. "Hurry up!"

"What is your *deal* today?" I asked. "Did someone give him espresso for breakfast again, because you know he's not supposed to drink that stuff."

"Don't look at me," Lucas said. "He woke me up before dawn. I figured he's an early riser."

"Not usually," I said. "We practically have to blast him out of bed with dynamite at home. Maybe it's the effect of all this fresh air."

I ate the rest of my breakfast under the rat's disapproving glare. By the time we were ready to start up to the house, Rodney was almost beside himself with impatience. He stood on the ice chest watching me brush my teeth with his arms crossed and one hind foot tapping out an annoyed rhythm.

"Are you trying to earn your ghost hunting merit badge?" I asked, with my mouth full of toothpaste. "'Cause I think

Darby might be able to give you some pointers on the subject."

I swear to you, he had the nerve to stick his tongue out at me.

Five minutes later, with the group assembled, I took down the barrier spell. We walked toward the house in a ragged line, with Festus ambling ahead, Rube waddling at his side. The rough plan was for the two of them to go into the house first, have a look around, and scout out the attic.

A strategy that elicited outraged protest from Rube.

"What is this? Sacrifice the people with fur first?"

In response, Festus made a sound that could have been an impending hairball or derision. Six of one half dozen of the other.

"I don't notice Rodney getting all cowardly about going up to the house."

From my shoulder, Rodney looked down on Rube with evident condescension.

"Just 'cause I got sense enough to be prudential like about going in there don't make me a coward," Rube said, puffing out his chest. "You're so tough, you lead off."

"My pleasure," Festus replied, which left Rube no choice but to accompany him.

At the porch steps, the werecat turned to Lucas, all traces of his usual wisecracking demeanor gone. "Hang back. Once we've checked out the attic, we'll give you the all clear."

"Got it. Be careful."

They were gone less than 15 minutes when Rube stuck his head out of the tall dormer window at the top of the house and yelled down. "Lucas, get up here!"

"What is it?"

"You're gonna have to see for yourself," Rube said. "Straight up the steps to the second floor, turn right, dinky staircase down at the end of the hall. We left the door open."

Before Lucas could ask for more information, the raccoon popped back inside.

We followed the raccoon's directions, spotting a line of paw prints in the dust on the second floor that led to an open doorway. The steps ascending toward the attic were steep with deep recesses worn in the center of the treads.

Climbing single file, we found Rube and Festus sitting on either side of a small chest. The lock had been pried open, and the lid rested at an odd angle.

"What is it?" I asked, still out of breath from our quick ascent of the stairs. "What did you find?"

Festus blinked his amber eyes slowly. "Look inside. Tell me what you see."

Leaning forward nervously, I peered into the trunk. Plush blue velvet lined the pristine interior. There, sparkling up at us, lay a crystal the size of a hen's egg set in an oval of rose gold. There were symbols etched in the metal with precise, black lines.

Power pulsated from the stone in waves that somehow felt familiar. In spite of Tori's caution to avoid touching objects and the incident with the candle, my hand reached toward the crystal.

Lucas stopped me, his fingers clamping down firmly on my wrist.

"I don't think that's a good idea. Those are Druidic runes."

"Can you read the inscription?"

He studied the markings. "They're ancient, but I think the rough translation would be 'rest within and wait for the resumption of time.' We'll have to get Moira to render the text more accurately."

"Raise your hand if you're wondering what a Fae artifact is doing in an abandoned house filled with hoodoo paraphernalia on land owned by a bunch of vampires," Tori said. "Anyone? Anyone?"

Connor's hand shot up, followed by Rube's paw and Festus' tail.

"Lucas, you're the artifact expert," I said. "What do we do?"

"We can't leave it here, Can you use your psychometry to get a read on the thing without letting it suck you in?"

"It's calling to me already, but I don't get the sense that it wants to hurt me."

"Famous last words," Tori muttered.

I shook my head. "I don't think so. This is going to sound crazy, but it's like the crystal knows me."

This time it was Festus who intervened. "You shouldn't explore this object here. We have an entire archive at our disposal back at the fairy mound and experts in this kind of thing. I say we close this chest and take it back to Briar Hollow."

Even though I felt an almost overwhelming urge to interact with the crystal, I knew he was right.

"Okay, but we came here to solve a specific problem for the Ionescus. We haven't done that."

Lucas, still staring at the crystal, shoved his hat back on his head. "Maybe I'm wrong, but I don't think you can figure that problem out until you understand this artifact."

In my heart, I knew he wasn't wrong. Whatever was in this house had to be tied to the Druidic stone. But here's the thing that did bother me. I knew I was tied to the stone as well.

Chapter Twenty-One

You know the line "there's no place like home?" When we hit Briar Hollow, not 36 hours after we'd left, and discovered everything that had happened in our absence, I almost wanted to go back to the haunted house.

Little did I know I'd brought back a souvenir from our excursion other than the crystal amulet nestled in the blue velvet interior of the chest.

First, we walked in the back door only to be more or less tackled by a stylishly attired young woman I could have sworn I'd never seen before in my life — until she started babbling a mile a minute.

"Glory?" I said, holding her at arm's length and studying her features.

She grinned and nodded, almost — but not quite — too thrilled to speak.

"I did it all myself, Jinx. I worked, and I worked, and I *worked* learning what the ingredients meant and how they should be mixed."

She wheeled on Tori. "And I am *ever* so sorry I didn't ask permission, but I didn't think you'd mind if it worked. And it did. Work. I'm big again! But Chase says I'm not big, that I'm really small, which I've *never* been in all my whole life, so I'm not just me again, I'm a *better* me!"

Festus, back to his ginger cat self, shook his head. "That's Dill Pickle, alright. I'd know that high-level of incoherence anywhere."

Without warning, Glory bent down, scooped him up in her arms, and kissed him square on the nose.

"Festus! You go right ahead and insult me all you want to. Nothing is going to ruin my mood, not even a grouchy, fat old cat like you."

Narrowing his eyes to slits, Festus hissed, "Put. Me. Down. *Now.*"

Rube, who was lounging by the back door, fell over laughing. "Karma just smacked your backside, McGregor," he cackled. "Now you're the one with his paws dangling in the air. Guess it ain't so funny now."

"I will deal with you later, Sewer Rat," Festus spat. "Just as soon as this overgrown gherkin *puts me down.*"

Glory obliged him, but not before kissing his nose again and ruffling the fur on his ears. As soon as his paws hit the hardwood, Festus stalked off toward the lair grumbling something about having to "bathe for a week to get the pickle stench" out of his fur — which only made Glory laugh harder.

Rube trailed after Festus hurling one insult after another. Tori took charge of Glory, saying, "Come on. Show me how you pulled off this miracle."

That's when I spotted the moms, Brenna, and Greer drinking in the espresso bar.

Notice I didn't say drinking coffee.

That's probably because there was a bottle of expensive single malt in the middle of the table. Thankfully, it was after 5 o'clock, and the store was closed. We don't have a liquor license, and I can't afford to be serving 1937 Glenfiddich to the public.

In fact, I can't afford 1937 Glenfiddich at all. It goes for about $20,000 a bottle, which meant the whisky was from Greer's private and highly exclusive stock. Not a good sign.

Lucas recognized the bottle, too. His eyebrows shot up. "Uh, come on Connor, let's take the chest downstairs and start pulling research material."

My brother's eyes tracked to the espresso bar. He took in the scene and instantly decided all indications pointed to retreat as the better part of valor.

"We'll be downstairs if you need us, sis," he said, pecking me on the cheek and following Lucas through the door.

Steeling myself for the worst, I walked into the espresso bar. "What happened?"

Mom picked up the bottle and poured a glass for me. "Have a drink, Norma Jean."

I'm 30 years old, and that was the first time my mother ever told me to take a drink, much less poured the liquor.

"Oh God," I said, falling into a chair. "Is Dad dead?"

"Not when I saw him last," Mom said, "although he might have had a heart attack before he got off the phone with the insurance company."

"Did your store burn down?" I asked, my mind leapfrogging from one disaster scenario to the next. We had just driven by the building, hadn't we? I thought it was still standing, but I didn't trust my memory.

"Drink," Mom ordered again.

I did as I was told. Even bordering on panic, I managed to appreciate the vague toffee flavor of the Scotch with a suggestion of cinnamon. The whisky went down smooth, igniting a warm fire in my stomach. As Mom intended.

As she told me the story, I could not believe what I was

hearing, but I didn't say anything until she got to the part about Gemma rolling the rented van to avoid hitting a deer.

"You almost got yourself killed trying to miss a *deer?*" I asked, thunderstruck at the recklessness of the dangerous, albeit humane, choice.

Gemma swirled the dark, walnut-colored liquid in her glass. "This wasn't any old deer. It was a white doe."

"Okay, a *rare* deer, but still."

"You're missing the point, Jinx," Brenna said. "The white deer was an omen."

Oh, terrific! More strange Fae lore. Precisely what we didn't need.

"An omen of what?"

"We're still working on that," Mom said, "but that isn't the most serious part. We weren't able to deliver Seraphina and Ioana to the Ionescus."

Behind me, Tori said in a strangled voice, "The Strigoi Sisters? What the *hell!*"

I kicked out a chair and shoved a glass toward her. "Have a drink. Trust me on this one."

Tori sat down and splashed some of the whisky in the tumbler. On the first sip, her face went pale. "Oh crap. This is the good stuff. We've got *serious* trouble, don't we?"

"Oh, yeah," I said, "and I think Mom is getting to the good part."

My mother's next statement did not disappoint.

"The caskets broke apart when the van rolled. Gemma thinks the levitation potion she used weakened the wood and the silver. Anyway, Seraphina and Ioana got out. We had no choice but to let them leave the area."

At that, Tori downed her whisky and instantly poured herself another glass.

"Exactly what do you mean by 'no choice?'" I said.

When I heard the rest of the tale, I understood, but that

didn't mean I had to like it. "You actually believe that Seraphina and Iona aren't going to feed on humans? Why on earth would you trust those two about anything?"

"I do believe them," Brenna said. "They are far more interested in finding Irenaeus and exacting their revenge on him. That desire will, for the time being, buy us time."

Which only left one loaded question to ask. "What did Cezar say?"

Gemma put her hand over her face. Mom looked away, and Brenna got busy pouring herself another drink. That left Greer.

"He expressed some displeasure," she said, with a twinkle suggesting mirth showing in her green eyes.

"And you think that's *funny*?"

"That is not what I find amusing. I am entertained by the change in his demeanor when we exchanged remarks on equal footing."

"Meaning?"

"She went all vampiric on his butt," Gemma said.

I thought she'd been covering her face because she was upset. I was wrong. She was laughing, too. Which touched my mother off, and then Brenna.

"You have got to be *kidding* me," I said, regarding all of them with horror. "The four of you pull off this stunt behind my back because you knew I would have a fit, which, behold, I am now having. Then you turn two homicidal, blood-sucking sociopaths loose on the world, and you're *laughing*?"

Wiping her eyes, Mom said, "Lighten up, Norma Jean. We know it's bad, but you should have seen Greer back Cezar down. It was a thing of pure beauty. She let all that lovely fire come into her eyes . . . "

"And then she raised the flight of the baobhan sith," Brenna chuckled. "There she stood, her hair flared out on the wind . . ."

"Don't forget the lightning," Gemma said. "That was the best part."

Greer remained impassive. "They exaggerate. I merely sought to remind Cezar that he was talking to an equal, not an inferior. The change in his attitude in the aftermath proved quite remarkable."

"Which was what?" I said.

"That he would leave the Strigoi Sisters to us," Mom said.

Like that was a good thing.

Which it was not.

At all.

"*So*," Mom said, in a forced let's-change-the-subject voice, "how did things go at the house?"

She was getting ready to find out I could drop a bombshell, too.

"Oh, peachy," I said. "The entity is most certainly not an ordinary ghost, and we brought home a glowing crystal necklace we found in the attic."

Do I know how to shut down a bunch of cackling women, or what?

I was feeling pretty smug about the way I'd turned the cards on them until I saw the look in Brenna's eyes.

"Is the stone as large as the egg of a chicken? Set in rose gold and surrounded by Druidic runes?"

With a sinking feeling, I said, "Uh, yeah. Lucas tried to decipher the inscription, he thinks it says . . . "

"*Rest within and wait for the resumption of time*," the sorceress whispered. "That necklace belonged to Adeline Shevington. We must contact your grandfather immediately."

SERAPHINA WIPED the blood from her chin with the back of

her hand, then cleaned the sticky substance away with delicate flicks of her tongue.

"You look like a cat, sister," Ioana giggled, licking her own crimson lips, "lapping up the strawberry cream."

Pausing to test the flavor of the blood on her tongue, Seraphina said thoughtfully, "Not cream. More like thick gravy."

"When can we kill a human?" Ioana asked brightly, grabbing hold of her sister's arm and dancing in place. "A nice fat human! One that's had lots of butter and cream to eat."

Seraphina shoved the animal carcass at her feet into the undergrowth, kicking leaves over the body.

"Patience, Ioana. The next time we drain the life force of a humanoid it will be wizard's blood."

"Will he taste sweet?"

"He will taste *powerful*. We will feed slowly on Chesterfield, siphoning his life in delicious drops while he begs for our mercy. Until then, sister, we must find another way to survive.

"But how?" Ioana whined. "I don't want to go hungry again, and I don't want to eat animal blood. It's not the same."

"I know," Seraphina agreed sympathetically, "but it has quenched our hunger for now and brought us back to ourselves. We must get out of these woods and find a base from which we will be safe. I hear the sounds of traffic on the highway. Let us find ourselves a chauffeur."

The two strigoi slipped through the darkened forest with preternatural speed, emerging from the cover of the trees on the shoulder of a mostly deserted highway.

Ioana looked up and down the road. "There's no one here," she said petulantly. "I don't like being outside this long."

"Patience," Seraphina said, her eyes on the spot where the pavement met the horizon. "There's a truck approaching. We need only wait a short time."

After five minutes, headlights appeared in the distance.

Seraphina calmly stepped into the road, standing completely still as the engine sound grew louder. The driver saw her at the last possible minute, slamming on his breaks and coming to a skidding halt just inches from her body.

The door of the cab flew open, and a heavyset man jumped out swearing. "Are you out of your damn mind, lady or just plain stupid? I almost squashed you like a bug."

"Lower your voice," Seraphina commanded, "and uncover your head in my presence."

The truck driver instantly fell silent, hastily snatching his cap off and holding it awkwardly in his big hands. His face went slack.

"I'm sorry," he said in a subdued voice that sounded distant and removed. Confusion filled his features. "Who are you?"

Ioana stepped out of the darkness.

"Can we feed on him, sister?" she asked, cocking her head to one side like a curious bird. "He smells fat."

Seraphina sniffed the air. "He does, doesn't he?" she said, wrinkling her nose. "But perhaps a trifle salty. What is your name, human?"

Still turning his cap round and round in his hands, the driver said, "Eddie."

"Do you have sleeping quarters in your truck, Eddie?" Seraphina purred seductively. "Some place where the three of us might be alone?"

A different kind of light came into the man's glassy eyes. "I sure do."

"Show me," Seraphina ordered. "But first, drive us some place where we won't be seen."

Several hours later, Ioana lounged on one side of the unconscious driver running her long fingernails across his balding head.

"Please can't I finish him off?" she asked. "I'm still hungry."

"You're always hungry," Seraphina said, going through the papers in the cab. "I told you, we cannot kill him, besides, he may be of use to us."

"I liked the man who owned the pizza restaurant before Chesterfield turned him into a pile of dust."

"That was inconvenient," Seraphina agreed absently. "Pete had the makings of a faithful minion."

She extracted a piece of paper, her eyes scanning the sheet. "Sister, do you see the mark of a needle on Eddie's arm, somewhere near the bend of the elbow?"

Ioana pulled up the man's sleeve and ran her fingers over the skin. "Yes, I see it. The wound is still open."

"He gave blood yesterday. I thought he seemed a bit empty. This is the paperwork from a blood bank. That could be our answer, Ioana. A place where humans willingly give blood."

Frowning, Ioana said, "But they won't just give it to *us*."

"They will if we get jobs there," Seraphina said. "Father always told us that our people survive among the humans by hiding in plain sight."

Still sniffing at Eddie's arm, Ioana said, "I miss father, even if he didn't appreciate our transformation."

"He tried to kill us," Seraphina said, her eyes glinting like shards of ice, "the way Chesterfield tried to kill us when he put us in those boxes. That's not going to happen again, sister. We will seek our revenge on the wizard, and then we will turn our attention to Kelly and Gemma."

Laughter bubbled from Ioana's throat.

"What amuses you so?" Seraphina asked.

"I bet Kelly and Gemma wish they'd never tried out for the cheerleading squad. We tried to tell them they don't have what it takes to play in our league."

Chapter Twenty-Two

The six of us got up to head for the lair minus one black and white rat. When I stood up from the table, Rodney ran down my arm, zig zagged through the whisky glasses and headed for the storeroom.

"You sure you don't want to come with us?" I called after him. "You know how you hate to miss things."

Without turning, Rodney waved a front paw over his head, which I interpreted to mean, "See you later."

"What's up with him?" Tori asked as we followed the other women toward the stairs.

"Beats me. He's been acting weird since breakfast. Maybe he needs a nap. None of us got much sleep last night."

"Speak for yourself. I slept like a rock, but if Rodney wants a nap, his condo is still in the lair. It's been there since the Freak Freeze. Why is he going to the store room?"

Under normal circumstances, I might have followed Rodney to see what scheme he'd cooked up now, but Brenna's announcement about the crystal pendant took precedence over our resident rodent's eccentricity.

As soon as we came down the stairs, I spotted the chest

holding the pendant. Lucas and Connor had put it in the center of the conference table.

Festus was sitting next to the box telling Chase, Glory, and Beau about our discovery, while Rube camped out on the other side interrupting him from time to time with corrections on key details.

The first words I heard out of the raccoon's mouth were, "I did *not* fly out of the house like a bat out of hell."

Festus started to give what would have no doubt been a sardonic reply when Beau noticed us.

"Welcome back, Miss Jinx," he said, his face lighting up in greeting. "From the account we are hearing, it would seem you all had a most fascinating excursion into the mountains."

"Hi, Beau. Doesn't look like you all were bored in our absence either."

"Indeed not. Miss Glory has been all but overcome with anxiety anticipating your return so that she might reveal her transformation."

Our newly enlarged friend glowed radiantly beside him. Normally that would mean she looked like an elated pistachio. Honestly, getting used to Glory's new complexion threw me more than the change in her size.

At the moment, any reference to her impressive accomplishment amounted to dropping a quarter into a woman who, even in her worst moments, embodied the definition of effusive. In her current state, Glory had rocketed past "gushing" and moved on to "erupting."

"I got big just in time to be really useful," she enthused. "Lucas says we need to figure out what this necklace is all about. I've got some ideas about sources we can consult . . ."

When I held up my hand, Glory stopped talking, and her face fell. "You don't want me to help?"

For months Glory had been campaigning for the right to participate more fully in events in the lair, assuming we thought her incapable of doing so because of her size. She immediately took my gesture that day as another diminishment of her talents.

"No, no," I assured her hastily. "That's not it at all. Brenna thinks she can identify the crystal already without any research."

All eyes turned toward the sorceress, who looked distinctly uncomfortable under our combined scrutiny.

"May I see the item so that I might be sure?" she asked.

"Of course," Lucas said, "it's right there in the chest."

We all watched as Brenna approached the box with wary steps. She stopped at the edge of the table and grew unnaturally still. When the silence stretched past the point of tolerance, Mom moved beside her, laying a hand on Brenna's back.

"What is it?"

Brenna tried to answer, but couldn't get the words out until she cleared the lump in her throat. "I was correct. This necklace belonged to Adeline Shevington."

"Are you sure?" Mom asked.

A fine tremor passed through Brenna's body. "Yes, Kelly.

I was there the night Adeline was murdered. I watched Irenaeus do it."

The implication of the statement stunned us all. We'd come to accept that Chesterfield murdered his sister in law, but it hadn't occurred to us that Brenna, his known associate at the time, witnessed the killing.

I began to put the pieces together. Chesterfield took the Amulet of Caorunn from Adeline that night, but Barnaby said the dying woman transferred her magic into a crystal amulet. That had to be the piece of Fae jewelry we'd found at the deserted house, but how in the world did it get there?

According to the story Barnaby told us, he held the amulet for safekeeping until he met his second wife, Adoette. Those details emerged during our attempt to recover the stolen

Amulet of Caorunn. With all our concentration on one piece of enchanted bling, we'd completely forgotten about the other.

"Why didn't Chesterfield take this necklace the way he took the Amulet of the Phoenix?" I asked.

"Because the crystal would not let him," Brenna said. "The stone grew so cold he could not lay his fingers upon it, yet the necklace rested on the skin of Adeline's body without marring her flesh."

Her words made it clear to me that Brenna didn't know how long the mortally wounded woman had survived.

"When that happened," I said. "Adeline wasn't dead. She lived long enough to tell Barnaby that she had transferred her magic into that stone to be passed on to a new Witch of the Oak."

The sorceress regarded me with stricken eyes. "I would like to believe that I would not have left my kinswoman to die on that cold floor had I known. Not even to follow Irenaeus' bidding."

Kinswoman?

"You were related to Adeline Shevington?"

"She was my cousin, which makes my actions that day in blind obedience to the curse of the Creavit and to Irenaeus Chesterfield all the more vile."

No one knew what to say to that until Greer quietly intervened. "Let us all sit. When we apprise Barnaby of the discovery of this necklace, I believe it would be to our benefit to be in command of the complete body of relevant facts."

Each of us claimed the nearest available chair. I hadn't seen Brenna's face look so strained since that first night she appeared in the mirror offering to help us rescue the Queen of Winter from Fer Dorich.

"Chase," I said, "would you pour Brenna a drink?"

When he handed her the glass, the sorceress took it with

shaking fingers. Something about that unnerved me more than her admissions about Adeline.

In the months Brenna had been in Briar Hollow, I'd come to genuinely care for her. Surrounded by family for the first time in centuries, the tentative woman who entered our lives had begun to radiate strength and good humor.

Apart from our conversation after the Freak Freeze, no one had forced Brenna to talk about the worst aspects of her dark history. Now the situation demanded she confront a particularly distasteful part of who she had been.

Don't ever believe that people can't change. They can, but often at the price of great personal pain. Brenna regrets her misdeeds to the depths of her soul. That day wasn't the last time she's had to lay bare her past so that we all might move forward.

Every time I watch her do it, my respect for the sorceress' unflinching courage grows. The hardest demon Brenna Sinclair will ever have to face is the one standing guard over her memories. I don't judge her because she's doing a fine job of judging herself.

Brenna thanked Chase and took a swallow of the whisky. Then casting her eyes toward the floor, she said, "This is not a tale I have wanted to share with you. I am afraid it will change the good opinion you've kindly formed of me."

Taking Brenna by the elbow, Mom steered her toward one of the couches and sat down beside her. She caught hold of the woman's free hand and commanded gently, "Brenna, look at me."

My heart lurched when I saw the fear in her eyes, but I stayed silent and let my mother handle the situation. Even during my growing up years, when Mom labored under the nervous fallout of the tragic events of her youth, she knew how to comfort someone else's worst fears.

I remembered how it had felt when she would come into

my room at night to quiet my terror over a nightmare. The way the edge of the bed sank under her weight before the cool touch of her fingers brushed the sweat stained hair back from my forehead.

"Hush, little girl," she'd whisper in the darkness. "It was only a dream. I'm here."

Now she spoke not to the Brenna Sinclair who had terrorized and manipulated the courts of Europe, but rather to the young girl Brenna had been when first she bargained with the darkness.

"None of us labor under the illusion that you didn't do horrible things when you were Creavit," Mom said, reaching out and wiping a tear from Brenna's cheek. "That was all in the past. We have forgiven you. This is your home now. You can tell us what happened the night Adeline died. We're not going to cast you out."

Brenna's lips quivered. "*You* might not, but Barnaby Shevington is another matter."

I moved to sit on the other side of Brenna, taking the glass of whisky from her and entwining our fingers. "Barnaby does not dictate what happens in Briar Hollow. So long as I am the Witch of the Oak, you have a home with us."

The sorceress smiled at me through her tears. "Thank you, but it is more than that. I . . . I don't want you — any of you — to think badly of me again."

"Brenna," Mom said, "if you don't tell us about the day Adeline died, you'll never be free of the guilt or this terrible fear. Passing through the fire between the realms reversed the Creavit spell. It didn't heal your real wounds. That's something you have to do yourself, and you have to trust us to help you. Tell us what happened."

Brenna gave a short nod, but she didn't turn loose of either of us. She told us that Chesterfield came to her in London where they were living at the time and invited her on an "outing."

"He said we were going to the country on an errand. He didn't say where, and I didn't ask. In those days, Irenaeus and I were intimate. I followed him without question because I believed that he loved me. That was the day I learned he loves no one but himself."

When they came out of the portal near Barnaby's country estate in Kent, Brenna grew suspicious. "Barnaby had taken the name Shevington, but there were wild rumors circulating that he was a Chesterfield. Some even went so far as to suggest Barnaby had a hand in touching off the Fae Reformation to further his position with the Ruling Elders."

Adeline answered the door and let them into the house. "We never went past the entrance hall," Brenna said, her eyes unfocused as she recalled the details of that day. "Irenaeus claimed that he was there to speak to Barnaby about negotiating a truce between the Hereditarium and the Creavit. Adeline didn't believe him. She ordered us out of the house, flinging the doors open with a wave of her hand."

Honor was the fatal flaw that sealed Adeline's fate. "She turned her back on Irenaeus. I don't think it entered her mind that a magical practitioner, even a Creavit, would attack another Fae from behind and without warning, but Irenaeus has no principles in that regard. He struck her with a bolt so intense it threw her across the room and into the wall. The force of the blow broke her back."

We listened in horror as Brenna described how Irenaeus dragged the injured woman into the center of the hall. "He wanted her to be on display when Barnaby returned home. He took the Amulet of the Phoenix from her neck and ripped open her dress to take the crystal as well, but the pendant rebuked him. We left her there on the floor. I had no idea she was still alive."

"Did you know she was pregnant?" I asked softly.

The tears in Brenna's eyes spilled over. "Not then. Irenaeus told me later. He said Barnaby had deprived him of his birthright and Irenaeus repaid the favor by killing Barnaby's only child."

"What a bastard," Gemma muttered darkly.

Brenna shook her head, releasing my hand to dry her wet cheeks. "You have no idea the depths of his bastardy, and I pray to the benevolent Universe you never find out."

After that, only the crackling of the fire broke the silence in the lair until Festus spoke. "I have a question."

"Of course," Brenna said. "What else can I tell you?"

Lifting one paw, he pointed toward the table. "Can you explain to us why the shiny magic rock is doing that?"

Chapter Twenty-Three

Sylvia floated suspended in the center of the storeroom talking with Rodney who sat on the shelf across from her.

"Little Brother, I do not know what to do to make my presence known to your mistress."

Rodney jumped from the shelf to the back of the couch and landed on the low coffee table next to an iPad. He pressed the home button on the tablet and swiped his paw to move past the lock screen.

Intrigued, Sylvia bent low over the device. "Is this a strange sort of book?"

Rodney waggled his paw back and forth indecisively.

"A book but not a book? How is that possible?"

He held his left paw up as if to say "wait," using the right to open a browser. Scampering back and forth, he typed in a phrase, selected an entry, and hit "search."

When the screen filled with words, he looked up questioningly at Sylvia.

"Yes, I can decipher the writing of humans. It was necessary for me to learn so that I might be of more help to Sam. What is it you are trying to tell me, Sir Rat?"

Rodney pointed to the screen.

Bending again, Sylvia read. *"There is a general skepticism about the reality of paranormal phenomenon. In the vast majority of cases, objective investigations have yielded no plausible proof that anything exists beyond the human world."*

Perplexed, Sylvia said, "But these people are Fae, they are not of the human world."

The rat held his paws out and waved them around in a wide circle.

"Look around me? What would you have me observe?"

Rodney repeated the waving motion and then tapped the side of his head.

"I know you wish for me to think. Are you trying to tell me that by living among the humans, the witch and her friends have developed a similar skepticism regarding events they cannot explain?"

Rodney nodded and typed on the iPad again. A live video image of the lair filled the screen.

"Where is this place?"

The rat pointed down.

"Under our feet?"

He nodded.

"I do not understand. Though he is in corporeal form, the aura of the older gentleman wearing the tall boots tells me he is a specter, as is his canine companion. How can your friends be skeptical and live in companionship with spirits?"

Rodney pointed to his eyes with two of his front toes, then pivoted and pointed at the screen. He repeated the move several times before she understood.

"Ah, they could see him before he became corporeal. They understand ghosts, but they know no creatures of my kind, is that correct?"

Rodney clapped his paws and gave her a thumbs up.

"So your friends came to the house I shared with Sam expecting a ghost and therefore looked only for a ghost. I must make them look for something more than that. You are quite clever, Sir Rat. Does your strange book contains suggestions about how I might redirect their thoughts?"

FOR THE RECORD, nothing that happened after the crystal started to glow can be blamed on me. I didn't light any candles while entertaining wayward intentions. I didn't touch an object without considering the psychometric ramifications.

I did nothing.

Nada.

Zip.

Like everyone else in the lair, I looked in the direction Festus pointed to see the box sitting on the table with light pulsating from its interior.

"Is that what it was doing at the house?" Mom asked.

"We didn't see the crystal glowing at the house," I replied, "but we did see flashes of light in the attic when we were camped in the yard. That's what Cezar told us got people interested in checking out the place."

When no one moved, Gemma said, "So are we going to sit here and watch it glow?"

"I ain't going over there," Rube said. "I went into that wacky shack first. I'm the one who got molesterized by the Petting Ghost. I ain't checking out no possessed pet rock. Count. Me. Out."

Festus shook his head. "Is a werecat's work never done?" he asked with a world-weary sigh. He hopped down from the hearth and started limping across the floor.

"Dad," Chase said, a note of warning in his voice, "are you sure that's such a great idea?"

The old cat flicked his tail in a way reminiscent of an entirely different gesture. "All my ideas are great, boy," he said, springing up on the table.

As we watched, he put his front paws on the lip of the box and looked inside.

"So what's it doing?" Rube asked.

"Glowing, you moron," Festus replied, "and there's something in the center of the stone that looks like a storm cloud."

I glanced over at Lucas. "What do you think?"

"The fairy mound should keep us safe. After all, this whole place is one big artifact containment center. I think it's okay to have a look."

"Right," Festus said. "Glad to have your professional opinion there Mr. DGI Big Shot. I notice you didn't come up with that assessment until a werecat led the way."

Chase turned his head so I wouldn't see him grinning, but it didn't work. He and Lucas may have negotiated a truce, but Chase is not above enjoying a joke at Lucas' expense, especially when Festus delivers the straight line with his trademark acerbic aplomb.

"Good enough for me," Tori said, pushing up from her chair. "Let's have a look."

From the expression on Connor's face, I could tell he had his doubts about the wisdom of getting closer to the crystal, but he followed Tori anyway.

One by one we all formed a ring around the table. Glory couldn't resist saying, "Oh my goodness this is so *awesome*! I can see something that's going on for a change without someone having to pick me up!"

"Brenna, any ideas about what it's doing?" Mom asked.

I heard, "*the crystal was used as a receptacle*" before a roaring sound drowned out the rest of the words.

"What the heck is that?" I asked.

Even though I thought I'd raised my voice, no one heard me. I tried again — louder this time — but still no reaction.

Then I realized the others were moving, but at a speed well under the kind of slow motion you see in the movies. I had the sense that my companions were in one stream of time and I was in another.

A sound from the crystal made me look down. The light inside continued to pulsate, but the shell of the stone cracked open allowing thick, yellowish smoke to form a hovering cloud.

"Uh, guys. *Hello?*" I tried again. "We've got a situation here."

When I still didn't get an answer, I moved to close the box, thinking that might be enough to stop whatever was trying to escape the crystal, but my body wouldn't cooperate.

Helpless, I watched the cloud elongate, rise in a column, and reach for me. I tried to hold my breath, but it didn't work. Slowly and steadily, the vapor flowed into my nostrils and disappeared.

Time snapped back to normal. Without the support of the temporary paralysis from which I'd suffered, I swayed on my feet. Lucas caught me.

"Did anybody else see that?" I asked, sagging against him.

"We saw," Chase said, "but we couldn't move, or at least I couldn't."

"None of us could," Mom said, putting her hands on my face and studying my eyes.

"See anything in there?" I joked weakly.

She stroked my temple comfortingly. "My girl. I see my girl. How do you feel?"

"I'm not sure. I think we need to call Grandad now."

With that, I passed out.

"NOTHING YOU HAVE TRIED WILL WAKE her?" Barnaby said.

"No," Kelly said. "Her heart rate and pulse are normal. She seems to be asleep, but she won't wake up. We've all tried."

The mayor of Shevington scrubbed at his face. "Victoria, was there anything in the house that identified its former occupant?"

"Yes," Tori said. "There were papers on the desk. His name was Sam Clinton."

Barnaby paled, a reaction that was not lost on Brenna. "You knew this man."

"I did," he admitted, "or I believe I knew his antecedents. When I gave the crystal pendant to Adoette, the magic of the Witch of the Oak transferred to her in much the same manner you described what happened to Jinx. The necklace remained in Adoette's possession until our daughter, Knasgowa, assumed guardianship of the Mother Tree. Knasgowa did not tell me why, but she gave the crystal into the care of a guardian named Nehemiah Clinton. He left Shevington, and I have heard nothing of him or his people since."

Beau spoke up. "Forgive me, Barnaby, but if the power attendant to the position of Witch of the Oak existed in the amulet and merged with your second wife, what remained in the stone that has now entered Miss Jinx?"

"I don't know, but Moira, Myrtle and I are on our way. Do not touch the stone in the interim."

The mirror connection broke before Barnaby could hear what Tori muttered under her breath. She was sitting on a chair next to the couch where Jinx lay sleeping, leaning her arms on her knees as she studied her friend's face for any sign of consciousness.

"Tori!" Gemma said. "Language."

"Whatever," Tori said darkly. "Am I the only one who

thinks we should have gotten a heads up on this crystal thingamajig?"

Lucas put his hands on her shoulders. "I'm worried about her, too, Tori, but jumping all over Barnaby when he gets here won't help."

"Okay, fine," she said, "but I'm glad Myrtle is coming with him. She'll know what to do."

"AOS SI, I really must protest this delay," Barnaby said. "My granddaughter is lying unconscious after an encounter with the very crystal that once housed my wife's magic. We must get to the fairy mound."

Myrtle regarded him with a placid expression that did nothing to help the Lord High Mayor's growing impatience.

"Do not forget that I love Jinx as if she were my own child, Barnaby. If I believed her to be in danger, I would not tarry. I must speak briefly with the Mother Tree. Excuse me."

As Myrtle walked away, she heard an explosive burst from Barnaby, soothed by Moira who said, "My love, trust the aos si and the Great Oak."

Stepping under the dark canopy of the massive tree, Myrtle sat on one of the benches at the base of the trunk and closed her eyes. Instantly her consciousness shifted from the busy world of the Shevington town square to the inner stillness of the Mother Tree.

"Did you feel it?" Myrtle asked.

The voice of the Oak resonated in her being. "I did."

"Did I speak the truth to Barnaby. Is Jinx truly free from danger?"

"No harm will come to Jinx Hamilton, but the return to the island that bears my name has begun."

"The reunion will cause pain to the Lord High Mayor and

to the Alchemist," Myrtle said. "They are both my beloved friends. I wish they could be spared this."

The Tree sighed. "It is a fallacy that love comes free of pain. The Mayor and the Alchemist will be tested, but they will not be damaged. Since the day I quit the old land to journey beneath the sea and begin anew in Shevington, I have waited for this day. Now go, old friend. Go and awaken the sleeping witch."

When Myrtle stepped back into the bright sunshine, she saw the carriage that would carry them to the portal had arrived from the stables. Ellis Groomsby himself sat in the driver's seat.

Barnaby held the door open, allowing first Moira and then Myrtle to enter. He started to climb in as well but stopped when Innis called to him from the front door.

"Blast and be damned!" he swore, going back to speak with her.

In the brief time they were alone, Moira said, "Did the Mother Tree tell you what has happened?"

"She only said that Jinx is in no danger."

"Thank the Universe for that," Moira said, staring over at the Tree with troubled eyes.

"What is it?"

Shaking her head, Moira said, "Only an idea that has come to my mind. Nothing that is possible."

The aos si did not answer, but if she had, she would have told the alchemist that the things that are most impossible are generally the first to see the light of a new day.

Chapter Twenty-Four

Drifting in a delicious, cool void, I felt relaxed and wonderfully removed from the problems of the Fae world. Far in the distance I could make out the emotions of the people I loved.

Currents of worry reached me, carried along on the threads that bound me to Tori, my mother, and Lucas, but the others were there as well. Chase's feelings came to me as a roiling mass of confusion.

I sensed the weight of Festus' paws as he paced back and forth on the hearth, and the nervous way Rube wrung his paws.

Rodney seemed farther away, still upstairs, perhaps, and curiously focused on a different set of worries. I thought he might be communicating with someone, but I couldn't understand the exchange.

I didn't want any of them to be upset, but curiously, I didn't want to go back either. This place was peaceful and set apart.

It wasn't until I heard Myrtle's voice that I felt compelled to answer.

"Jinx, you must wake up now. Follow my voice to the surface. You are needed."

Sighing, I kicked upward through the liquid fog, not quite swimming, but not flying either. A pinprick of light appeared over my head, growing larger with each movement of my legs until, with one final surge, I came awake. The transition was so jarring I sat up with a strangled cry.

Tori held my hand tightly, and my mother's arm was instantly around me. Lucas was there, too, and behind him, Chase.

"How long have I been out?"

"Better than an hour," Mom replied. "How do you feel?"

The rapid thundering of my heart had begun to slow, and I was no longer struggling for breath. I thought about the soft, comforting place where I'd been resting.

"Honestly? I feel like I had the best nap in the world."

Mom laughed, but the sound was tense and nervous. "Well, Norma Jean, I'm glad you enjoyed yourself because you scared us half to death. Moira, don't you think you should have a look at her?"

The tall alchemist appeared behind my mother. "I do, but I am afraid you will have to move aside, Kelly."

Mom reluctantly released me and stood back from the couch, but not too far away. Tori squeezed my hand. "You good?" she mouthed.

When I nodded, Tori released me and gave Moira my chair. Barnaby appeared over her shoulder.

"Wow," I laughed, "you guys really called out the big guns, didn't you?"

Moira, who had been feeling of my neck, said, "Eyes forward please."

When I did as I was told, she frowned and leaned closer. All the blood drained from her face.

"Is it that bad?" I asked uneasily.

Still studying me intently, the alchemist whispered, "Is it really you?"

"I am here," I answered, but my voice didn't sound right in my head. I was speaking in stereo.

Moira laid her hands on my arms, her fingers holding me tightly. "How is this possible?"

In my awareness, I seemed to step aside while someone else answered her.

"Because you remembered to take me to our people," the voice said. "Moira, you were then, and you are now, my dearest friend. You have cared well for him, even when he did not care for himself."

The words tore a gasping sob from Moira's throat. "Adeline?"

"Yes."

IN THE LANDSCAPE of my thoughts, my inner eye opened. I was standing in a room not unlike the lair, but filled with objects from my life — stuffed animals from childhood, school-books, a closet full of favorite outfits, my waitress uniform.

Turning in a circle, I took in the shelves that brimmed with books and photo albums. In the center of it all, a fire burned brightly in an open fireplace. There, all the cats I've ever known and loved snoozed contentedly on a thick, Oriental rug.

A woman sat beside the hearth in the chair from my child-hood bedroom. One of my first cats, Mr. Whiskers, sprawled across her lap purring.

"We share a common love," she said. "We are both ailurophiles."

Summoning all my eloquence, I answered. "Huh?"

She laughed. "We love cats. Barnaby used to get quite put

out with me when I would take in another, but after I died, he protected them as I had. Come, sit with me."

I didn't feel myself move. One moment I was standing across the room from her and the next I was sitting in the rocking chair that belonged to old Mrs. Lewis who lived next door to us when I was little. I loved that chair and had been searching for one like it for years.

As if following the connections I was making, the woman explained what was happening to me.

"We are in the space of your memories. You've never found that rocking chair, but it exists clearly in your mind. You've had a good life so far, Jinx. You are filled with love for your family and friends."

"Who are you?" I croaked. "And what are you doing in my head?"

"My name is Adeline."

"Adeline Shevington?"

"Adeline Moore Shevington, but my mother was a Sinclair."

"Are you here because of Brenna?"

"Brenna is only a part of the events that brought me here. The story is a long one. You might want to pick up a cat and get comfortable."

For as appealing as that idea sounded, I said, "But the others are waiting for me to say something."

"You will speak in less than a heartbeat in their reality. You and I are conversing at the speed of thought."

"Then we're in trouble. I've never been a quick thinker."

Adeline waved her hand toward the ceiling, which disappeared to reveal a dense network of interconnected cables all pulsating with light.

"That isn't true. You have an excellent mind. Strong. Resilient. Resourceful. Constantly growing in depth and understanding."

"Thank you, but I have no idea what's happening now. Are you the yellow smoke that rose out of the crystal?"

"None of us are the bodies we inhabit. They are but vessels for what is true and enduring. At the moment of my betrayal by Irenaeus Chesterfield, I transferred that essence, along with my magic, to the stone."

"But Barnaby says you spoke to him."

"I did, in his mind as we are speaking now, but his grief was so overwhelming, he believes my physical body still contained life in that moment. Please give this information to Brenna. I do not want her to live with the guilt of thinking she abandoned me while I still had life in my body."

That was a little too gracious to be believed in my book.

"Don't you blame her for not stopping him?"

Adeline shook her head. "I'm sure it's quite difficult for you to understand, but no, I do not. You will learn more of the story of the Sinclairs in the weeks ahead. For now, please grant me this favor."

Weeks ahead? This was not sounding like a temporary arrangement. Then I realized I was thinking while I was thinking all of this, which was also a thought...

"Don't. There is no need to try to impose logic on the mystery of the paradox that allows us to share this space. Simply accept it and believe me when I tell you that I wish you no harm. There is a task we must perform together and then this period of our relationship will end, and another will begin."

That didn't make sense either, but at least I was getting a rough time limit on my crystal-induced case of multiple personality disorder.

"Why *are* you here?"

"We will go to London together," she said, stroking Mr. Whisker's glossy fur and smiling indulgently into his upturned face.

As quickly as the words were out of my mouth, I knew they weren't true, but I said them anyway. "I'm not going to London."

"Ah," Adeline laughed, "but you already know that you . . . that we . . . are going. May I suggest that you let me be the one to tell my husband about the change in plans?"

Her husband?

Who was also my grandfather?

Ewwwwwwww.

This time Adeline laughed so hard, Mr. Whisker's almost jumped down in protest. As she resettled the indignant cat in her lap, she said, "No, it won't be like that at all. You will not be privy to my memories in a way that will make you feel uncomfortable or violated. When I need to speak with Barnaby, it will be as if you have gone into another room for a few minutes, which is, I'm afraid, what I must ask you to do now."

That was fine with me. Grandad was not going to be happy over the change of plans. I was perfectly happy to miss his reaction first hand. "Go for it," I said, reaching for Mr. Whiskers. "Let me know when it's my turn."

ADELINE TRACED the lines of the alchemist's face with her eyes. "The years have been kind to you, Moira. I always envied your elven blood."

Answering in Elvish, Moira said, "If it is truly thee, tell me how we met."

Responding in the same tongue, Adeline said, "By the brook, deep in the woods when we were but girls. You had called the dragon flies to dance for you."

They reached for one another at the same time, embracing tightly. "How I have missed thee," Moira said, still using her native language. "Can you forgive me for loving him?"

"Forgive you? I bless thee for the love that restored him to sanity. I am happy for thee."

Behind them, Barnaby cleared his throat. "Moira, what has happened?"

The two women released each other. Adeline looked at her husband and asked Moira mischievously, "He still has not mastered Elvish?"

"He has not. His attempts amount to butchery."

"Good. We are still free to speak our minds in front of him, and he will be none the wiser." Then, sobering, she said, "We are confusing them all terribly, Moira. We will have time together later, dear one. Now we must labor through the long explanations."

Switching to English, Adeline said, "Please do not be concerned. Jinx is perfectly fine and happily preoccupied at the moment with the memory of a well-loved feline."

"Which one?" Kelly asked.

"Mr. Whiskers. A handsome fellow with orange fur not unlike Master McGregor's."

"And you are?"

Barnaby spoke before Adeline could answer. "She is my wife," he said in a choked voice. "It is you, isn't it, Adeline?"

"Yes, Barnaby, and I think perhaps you and I should speak in private for a moment. Jinx has suggested we use her alcove."

Chapter Twenty-Five

They sat only feet apart, but the distance between them stretched beyond time and space. As Jinx had suggested she do, Adeline pulled the soundproof curtain closed so they would have privacy. At first, she waited for him to speak, but Barnaby only looked at her until at last she broke the silence.

"You must say something, Barnaby if we are to make progress between us."

"I cannot begin to describe the sense of dislocation I feel," he said. "Gazing upon your face I see my beloved granddaughter, but your eyes tell me otherwise."

Catching hold of his hands, Adeline said, "The events that began on the night of our parting are coming full circle, my husband."

"I don't understand."

"At this juncture, you need know nothing more than my true identity. Do you doubt who I am?"

"No. I would know you in any form and in any place."

"On the night that you came home and found me, I transferred far more than my magic into the crystal."

For the first time, Barnaby smiled. "Adeline, though I may not be as young as I was then, I have hardly lost my senses. You do not need to state the obvious."

The sound of her laughter relaxed the tension in his body. "Why did you not tell me?"

"Because you would have sought a way to make me live again, and that is not how magic on this level works. Adoette sensed immediately what the crystal held, and in time she shared that secret with Knasgowa. The Cherokee witches were powerful seers. They foresaw much of what would come in the future and wisely secreted me away until the day when a heart called to me. Jinx possesses that heart."

"Why are you here? Surely you cannot mean to lay claim to this child's life."

"Of course not. Do not even think such a thing. Jinx will help me accomplish my purpose and then the relationship I share with her will change. In the meantime, we must come to London with you for the Conference of the Realms. On this, dear husband, I will brook no argument."

WHEN BARNABY and I stepped out of the alcove, everyone in the lair looked at us questioningly. I held up my hand and wiggled my fingers in greeting.

"That's Jinksy," Tori said. "Right?"

"Right, and there's been a change in plans. I'm going to London for the Conference of the Realms. Connor, you're running Shevington while we're gone. Right now, I'm going to bed. Grandad will fill in the details for everybody."

Maybe these declarations were abrupt, but I was tired and overwhelmed. I didn't have any energy left for diplomacy. I guess they all figured that out because no one tried to stop me.

Well, almost no one. Lucas caught me at the top of the stairs.

"Hey," he said, "I get it that you've had a long day, but I need to know you're okay."

In response, I stepped into his arms and laid my head on his chest. We stood there in the half-light holding each other for long minutes until I pulled away and looked into his eyes.

"You need to get back down there and help Grandad get everything ready."

"Okay, but what are you going to do?"

"Like you said, it's been a long day, and I now have a houseguest in my head. I'm going to get in my pajamas and introduce Adeline to 21st-century comfort food. There are chocolate chip cookies and milk in our future."

Leaning closer, I kissed him. "I need some space, okay?"

"I'll be down here if you need me."

SOMETIME AFTER MIDNIGHT, Tori knocked on the door of my apartment. When I opened it, she was standing there with two pints of Double Chocolate Crunch ice cream in her hands.

"We need spoons," she said, brushing past me and plunking down on the couch.

When the cats heard her voice, all four trotted out of the bedroom. As I went into the kitchen to get spoons, I heard her say, "No can do, guys. This is chocolate. It's bad for you. Next time I'll bring vanilla."

After I handed her a spoon and accepted my pint, I flopped back down in my chair. We ate silently for a couple of minutes before Tori said, "So, who am I talking to here?"

"Who do you think you're talking to?" I asked crossly.

"Just checking, Jinksy. You do have an Elizabethan English chick hanging out in your noggin."

"Yeah, I do, and Adeline says to tell you she likes your sense of humor."

"Tell her I said thanks," Tori replied, licking her spoon. "So is that how it works? She tells you to say something, and you say it."

In my head, Adeline asked politely, *"May I?"*

"Sure, go ahead."

When an English accent came out of my mouth, Tori jumped a foot eliciting a protesting yowl from Winston, who had been napping on her ankles.

"Apologies, Tori," Adeline said, "but Jinx was kind enough to let me speak for myself for a few minutes."

Still looking rattled, Tori said, "Where does she go when you do that?"

"She is here with me, reposing amongst her memories. Since her inner eye opened, she has accessed thoughts and images that have been lost to her for years. I am to tell you that you still owe her $50 for the blouse of hers you ruined in high school."

"Oh my God!" Tori exclaimed. "Would you just get over that Jinksy . . . "

Adeline regarded her with amusement. "She heard you, but I will let her repeat her characterization of your self-defense."

"This," Tori said, "is un-freaking-believable. So there's two of you in there?"

"For now, but I have no intention of intruding on Jinx's privacy. You are free to share confidences with her as you always have. I will not eavesdrop."

"Thanks," Tori said, "I appreciate that. So how long are you staying?"

"As I explained to Jinx, she and I must attend the Conference of the Realms in London. Matters that began long ago, culminating in my death are coming to a head. At the conclusion of the conference, I have other plans for my future. I wanted to speak with you in person to spare Jinx the tedium of repeating my every comment."

"Good call," Tori said, "she can be cranky when her patience runs out."

Adeline tilted her head to one side as if listening, laughed, and said, "I will be stepping aside now so that Jinx may share her colorful response with you. You are a good friend to her, Tori Andrews. Jinx has few memories that do not bear your imprint."

Tori tapped the side of her head and grinned. "Ditto for what goes on in here."

"Moira is that kind of friend to me," Adeline said. "It is a most special bond. Guard it well."

"With my life."

I looked at her and cocked an eyebrow. "Going all mushy on me will not get you out of hot water for that crack about me getting cranky."

"And we're *back!* Dig into that ice cream. Adeline let it get all melty."

YOU'D THINK that having the spirit of a dead woman take up residence inside my head was problem enough, but that's not how things work in my world. I came downstairs the next morning resolved to make the best of this situation until we left for London only to find Tori sitting in the espresso bar with a defiant brownie.

"Uh oh," I said, pouring myself a cup of coffee. "Do I even want to know what this is about?"

"Good morning," Tori said. "You're here just in time to talk some sense into him."

"Talk some sense into him about what?" I said, joining her at the table.

"He informed me he has no intention of quitting his part-time job as a haunt for hire," she said, taking a bite out of her doughnut. "He's all yours."

Groaning inwardly and resisting the urge to put my head in my hands, I said, "Darby, three days ago you didn't want any part of impersonating a ghost, and now you're telling us you won't stop?"

"I cannot stop, Mistress. Doing so would be shirking my responsibilities."

From somewhere in the back of my mind, I heard Adeline laugh. *"What's so funny?"* I asked her.

"He reminds me of the brownie who was the head of my household." I have no doubt he will respond to you with what he considers impeccable logic."

The lady knew her brownies.

"Okay, you not only won't quit, you can't?" I said. "Would you mind telling us why?"

"They need me, Mistress."

When he didn't bother to elaborate, I made a shooing motion with my hand. "Go on. Explain."

"They are most inefficient, Mistress. Even more than you are."

That did it. Tori, who had done an admirable job of using her serious grownup face to that point in the conversation, collapsed into a fit of laughter. Adeline wasn't the only one enjoying the brownie's recalcitrance.

"Exactly what are you doing over there at the Pike house," I asked suspiciously.

Drawing himself up to his full two-foot something, he said, "I am assisting them in the production of the video that will make their careers. They refer to me as the 'Tacogeist.' Master

Nick thinks they should apply for something called a kookie right on the term."

"Copyright," Tori snickered, making no effort to get control of herself.

Darby explained that after the taco levitation incident during his trial run at the house, he got the bright idea on the second night to twirl "Rupert's cube."

"I think you mean Rubix cube," I said. "What else?"

"After Mindy, Nick, and Kyle went to bed, I took the liberty of straightening up their living quarters."

My jaw dropped. "You *cleaned house* for them?"

"Not nearly so thoroughly as I clean this house, mistress," Darby said loyally. "I reserve my best work in your service."

Tori caught my eye. She didn't need to say a word for me to understand her meaning. *What are you gonna say to that?*

Opting to try some logic of my own, I said, "Darby, you do understand that we don't want Mindy, Nick, and Kyle to know about everything magical that goes on in Briar Hollow, right?"

"Oh, yes, mistress," he said, nodding earnestly. "I know the humans cannot find out about the ghosts or the werecats or the Fae or anything that goes on here."

Okay. That was at least one worry off the table.

"So how can it be a good thing for you to continue making them think they have a ghost in their house?"

"It makes them happy, Mistress, and when they are occupied with me, they do not look for the real ghosts."

Which was the argument we used to get him to take on the job in the first place.

"But Darby, what if they find out about you?"

"That will not happen, Mistress. None of the devices they use to look for ghosts work on me. I will not make a mistake like the one Duke made."

Remember that baseball game video I told you about?

Yeah, Duke charged the camera with teeth bared and went viral as The Hellhound of Briar Hollow.

"Exactly how long are you intending to keep going over there?"

Technically, I could have forbidden him to leave the store, but I don't operate that way, and the brownie knew it.

"I would like to continue visiting until they have posted their next video. They are already worried they will not have an additional 'monkey shot.'"

Even though I'm used to Darby's garbled terminology, I had to look to Tori for a translation.

"He means a money shot."

"I don't get it," I admitted.

"Let me guess," Tori said. "They're opening with the levitating taco, but they're worried they're not going to get something for a big finish. You want to go back and make sure they have a slam bang ending for the video."

Darby beamed at her. "You understand *perfectly*, Mistress Tori."

"Once they have their money shot, you'll stop?" I asked. "Promise?"

He held up his hand. "On my word of honor, Mistress."

Reluctantly, I agreed that he could go back, a decision that sent him bouncing off down to the lair to tell Glory and Rodney the good news.

"I don't think I like this," I told Tori as we watched him go.

"Look at it this way. As long as he's keeping them busy at their place, they're not going up to the old house, which is a good thing since we're not finished up there."

Which brought to mind the thing I had to do that I really, really, *really* didn't want to do. Report to Cezar Ionescu.

I had no doubt he was going to give me an ear full about the Strigoi Sisters, and I couldn't even respond with, "*Yeah, I know, but we fixed your haunting.*"

"Do you think I could get away with sending Cezar an email?" I asked Tori.

She looked at me like I had sprouted a second head. "Not even close. You're going to have to talk to him. For one thing, when we do figure out what the heck is haunting that place and get rid of it, somebody is going to have to clean out that house. There is no way we can leave all that hoodoo stuff lying around."

Before I could get around to making that call, however, we realized something that changed the content of the impending conversation — the ghost came home with us.

Chapter Twenty-Six

As we were getting ready to open up, Tori said, "Hey, thanks for cleaning up the whisky glasses we left in here last night."

"You're welcome, but it wasn't me. Darby must have done it."

Tori frowned. "I don't think so. He didn't get in from the Pike House until after you went upstairs. He fixed a midnight snack for everyone down in the lair before he went to bed."

"Must have been one of the moms then."

"Yeah, I guess so," Tori said, but she still had a puzzled look on her face.

That was our first hint that something wasn't quite right in the store — or maybe I should say something *else* wasn't quite right.

Around noon, I made a remark to Tori that we really needed to straighten out the essential oils case and get everything back in alphabetical order — only to watch in horror as the bottles started to rearrange themselves.

"Adeline, knock it off," I hissed internally, using my body to shield the display from the prying eyes of our coffee drinkers.

"Excuse me?"

"Thank you for wanting to pitch in, but we can't have this kind of thing going on in front of the humans."

I had the odd sensation that someone else was looking at the world through my eyes as if we were both standing at the same window gazing out.

"I'm not doing that," Adeline said, *"and there is no aura of magic around the motion of the bottles."*

"Meaning what?"

"Something is physically repositioning the containers."

"Is it a ghost?"

I assume she wanted a closer look since my body leaned toward the case and my eyes narrowed.

"I don't believe so, but a specter is a possibility."

Tori came up beside me. "Are you talking to your imaginary friend again?" she asked, pitching her voice under the hum of conversation from the espresso bar.

"Oh God," I whispered back, "was I talking out loud?"

"That would have been less weird than you standing here cocking your head to one side like you're listening to an invisible person. You're gonna have to watch that."

"Understood, but I was trying to make sure no one was watching *that*."

Tori leaned around me to look where I was pointing in time to see a bottle of Lemon Grass serenely float up from its incorrect position between Sandalwood and Peppermint to nestle in after Lavender.

"You're not doing that?"

"Tori, really? Of course I'm not doing it, and I wish whoever is doing it would stop already."

No sooner were the words out of my mouth than the bottle of Tea Tree Oil that had been moving out of the top shelf shoved itself back in, and all activity in the display stopped.

"Cooperative little sucker whatever it is," Tori muttered.

"Ask it to move something," Adeline said. *"As a test."*

Glancing over my shoulder to make sure no one was watching us, I said, "Could you put the bottle of Frankincense on the table, please?"

In response, the container slid off the shelf and glided down to land gently on the flat surface.

"Well, would you look at that," Tori said. "It's listening to you."

"It is," I said thoughtfully, "but why can't we see it? We've never had any trouble seeing ghosts before."

The Frankincense bottle quietly replaced itself. As we watched, three others left their spots and lined up on the table: Neem, Agar, and Ginger.

"Does that combination mean anything to you?" I asked Tori, expecting her to give me some kind of alchemical answer.

Instead, she said, "The oils don't, but the letters do: N.A.G. Not a ghost."

"Maybe," I conceded, "or it might be calling me a nag."

Tori wisely refrained from commenting about that.

After we closed the store, we all gathered in the espresso bar to discuss our visitor. Since none of the other witches could come up with another explanation, Tori's interpretation of the letters N, A, G was as good a theory as any.

"If it's not a ghost," Beau said, "what else could it be?"

"Many things," Brenna replied. "Darby has the power of invisibility, as do many inhabitants of the In Between. Perhaps our guest cannot manifest physically in this realm and so is trying to communicate with us in another way."

Connor snapped his fingers so loudly we all jumped. "I've got it! Use the fairy mound to expose the mystery guest."

"How do we do that?" I asked.

"You told me that there's a special kind of boundary spell on the stairs leading down to the basement, right?"

I nodded. "It's a sort of glamour-based security system.

Anyone who isn't on the list of people allowed down there will go into the real, physical basement, which is a complete disaster. The rest of us step through and go to the lair."

"Right," he said, "and the lair exists in the fairy mound which is an energy source."

Tori sat up. "Oh my God. I know where you're going with this. Amplification. Right?"

My brother nodded. "Just like with Duke."

"Okay you two geniuses," I said, "you want to give the long version for the slow folks in the room?"

"They don't need to," Gemma spoke up. "I know exactly what they mean. If you came back from that house with something attached to you that none of us can see, it should be amplified into visibility by the power of the fairy mound. That's how Duke becomes solid enough to touch in the lair, even though he's a ghost hound."

The theory made sense, but I wasn't the one who cast the barrier spell. I only knew how to add names to the list for approved access. When I pointed that out, Mom said, "That's easy. I'll go down to the lair and place a mirror call to Myrtle. She's in the Valley today, but she should be able to tell me what we need to do to make this work."

While Mom was out of the room, I complimented Connor on his idea. Blushing, he said, "I like to solve problems. There's usually a solution right in front of people's eyes; they're just too caught up in the hard part to see the thing that's easy."

"You're going to do a fantastic job running Shevington while we're out of town," I said, a compliment that only made him blush redder.

"I hope so. You could have given me some warning on that one."

"Sorry," I apologized, "yesterday wasn't my best day."

We were still talking about his newfound responsibilities as

Mayor Pro Tem of Shevington when Mom came back with a notebook in her hand covered in arcane hen scratching.

When she set the book down on the table, I peered at it, trying to make sense of the notes. Brenna, however, seemed to be following perfectly.

"A wise precaution," she said, studying the page like she was deciphering a scientific formula — which I guess she was. "Myrtle has added a containment element to the opening spell."

"Yes," Mom said, pointing to a couple of lines, "here and here. We take the barrier down long enough for Norma Jean to enter. The fairy mound will alert us when the entity goes through and will contain it in a separate bubble as the barrier slips back in place."

Brenna nodded. "Elegant. I know the aos si relies primarily on her native powers, but she is a poet of spellcraft."

"She is," Mom agreed. "Look at the syntax of the opening stanza."

The two of them sounded like a couple of movie critics pouring over one of those art house films with subtitles no one understands.

"They are correct," Adeline said. *"The aos si writes poetic enchantments."*

"Uh, excuse me?" I said. "Could we have a less admiration and a lot more action? I want to find out about our uninvited guest."

At the word "uninvited," a stack of paper napkins flew off the counter and flew across the espresso bar.

I held my hands up. "My bad. I didn't mean uninvited. I meant to say as yet unidentified."

Since nothing else went hurtling across the room, I took that to mean my apology had been accepted.

While the others stood back, Brenna, Mom, and Gemma

stood in a loose circle around the basement door. I opened the door and looked at them for instructions.

"Just stand there for a second, honey," Mom said. "We have to do the opening spell. Myrtle suggested the three of us do it together."

She held the notebook out in front of her. With Gemma and Brenna looking over her shoulder, the three women chanted several lines in Latin. I couldn't see that anything, in particular, had happened, but Mom gave me the go ahead to start downstairs.

I made it about six steps down when the fairy mound started flashing like a '70s disco. From the floor of the lair, Festus looked up from yet another card game with Rube, Leon, and Marty.

"What the *hell* are you doing up there?" he asked.

"Stay where you are," I warned him. "We're catching non-ghosts."

Behind me, I heard the trio at the top of the stairs chanting again. The light show stopped, and everything grew quiet. The three raccoons were still looking up at me, but their eyes had gone huge and round.

Festus, on the other hand, was his usual impassive self. "It worked," he said nonchalantly flicking his tail back and forth.

"It did?" I asked uneasily.

"It did. The non-ghost is standing right behind you."

Chapter Twenty-Seven

The ghosts I'm used to, look like . . . well, themselves. When I met Beau, he wore the Confederate uniform he died in. Howie, our late mayor, was a cheap suit kind of guy in life, a fashion sense he took to the grave and beyond.

The entity standing — or floating — behind me looked properly ethereal, but it wasn't a ghost. Frankly, she looked like a fairy, except all the fairies I know are six inches tall. The creature I stared at was more like six feet, although we've since discovered she expands and contracts to meet the needs of the moment.

Above us, the basement door opened. Mom came through first, stopping inside the barrier. Behind her, I heard Gemma say, "Did it work?"

"It worked."

"Well get out of the way so we can see!"

"Hold on," she replied. "The staircase is full at the moment."

Obligingly, the entity flowed over the banister and down

into the lair, scattering three raccoons into the stacks before coalescing beside the poker table.

Festus, complacent as ever, leaned over the table and examined the cards his opponents had discarded during their hasty escape.

"I knew Marty was bluffing," he said scornfully looking up and taking notice of the new arrival.

"Hey," the werecat drawled.

"Hello," the being answered, the word singing in the air like a clear, high note from a flute.

I stumbled down the last few steps and stood beside Festus. Out of the corner of my eye, I spotted Rube peering at us from under Beau's desk, but Marty and Leon were long gone.

Mom and the others trooped down the stairs and gathered behind me.

"Wow," Tori said, "that is not what I expected."

The being swirled in her direction. "Would you like me to assume a different form?"

Taken aback, Tori stammered, "Uh, no. Just be yourself. While we're on the subject what . . . er, who . . . are you."

"I do not know the word for what I am in your language."

Brenna stepped forward. "You are a sylph, an air elemental from the Middle Realm."

The sylph's body clouded over. "Are you going to send me back into exile?"

As usual with a bunch of Fae, the conversation was moving too fast for my tastes.

"Slow down," I said. "Let's start with your name."

"The human with whom I shared a home called me Sylvia."

The words from Sam's notebook came back to me. *"Sylvia came today, and now everything will be all right."*

Motioning to the others to sit down, I said to the sylph, "You lived with Sam?"

Waves of melancholy rippled through her form. "Poor Sam. So many clouds in his mind no wind could blow away."

Sylvia might not know the word "dementia," but she certainly understood its devastating effects.

"How did you come to leave the Middle Realm and serve as his companion?" Brenna asked.

Sylvia floated closer to the fire, pointing at the flames. "He called me with those, but smaller, in the containers you call candles. Sam wished to speak to his father. I came instead."

"Hoodoo," Tori said. "He must have tried an ancestor summoning spell. Given his state of mind, something went wrong, and the magic reached across the realms."

The sylph nodded. "Many things Sam intended went awry. I stayed and tried to assist him. It is the way of my kind."

I looked at Brenna, our resident Middle Realm expert. "What does she mean?"

"Sylphs are helper spirits. They are benevolent empaths and companions. When she realized the old man's state of mind, it would not have been possible for her to abandon him. Such an act is not in her nature."

In confirmation, Sylvia said, "I helped Sam until death freed him from his prison, but the remnants of his magic and my own apprehension prevented me from returning to my original place of incarceration. I lived alone in the house until you came and bade me come here with you."

Under her breath, Tori said to me, "Told you it was your fault. Guess you'll pay more attention the next time you light a candle, huh?"

"LEDs," I whispered back, "nothing but LEDs from now on."

In my mind, Adeline said impatiently, *"You are missing the most important thing the sylph has said to you, that she could not bear the idea of returning to her own prison. Pursue that line of inquiry."*

Gotta say, having an internal prompter? Makes a girl look *way* smarter than she really is.

"What did you mean when you said you couldn't bring yourself to return to your prison?" I asked Sylvia.

Before the sylph could answer, Brenna said quietly, "She means that she did want to live in exile like the other *nonconformi.*"

"Now," Adeline said, *"we get to the heart of the matter."*

To my shock, as Sylvia and Brenna took turns explaining the real nature of the Middle Realm and the Agreement I'd promised Fer Dorich would be lifted, we learned that the whole arrangement had been put in place as an act of segregation.

During the confusion of the Fae Reformation, with the Creavit playing power politics throughout the courts of Europe, the Ruling Elders realized that keeping humans from discovering the existence of magic could no longer be entrusted to the conscience of individual Fae.

"I'm afraid Irenaeus and I both had a great deal to do with that realization," Brenna conceded regretfully. "We were in no way circumspect in our use of magic or our manipulation of mortals to achieve our desired ends. Witches and wizards can and do, however, pass easily as humans."

"But gryphons like your friend, Aquila and air elementals like Sylvia cannot," Beau said. "Therefore they presented a greater risk to the order the Ruling Elders sought to restore."

"Exactly," Brenna said, "so Reynold Isherwood came up with a solution."

From the stacks, Greer said, "More specifically, a two-pronged solution."

She and Lucas walked into the lair. Neither one of them so much as blinked at the sight of the sylph floating in front of the fireplace.

"Where have you two been?" I asked.

"London," Lucas replied. "Barnaby sent us there to renegotiate the composition of the Shevington delegation to include you. While we were in town, we did some private research."

"Into what?"

Greer supplied the answer. "Reynold Isherwood's unaccountably foul state of mind. He is adamantly opposed to the dissolution of the Agreement. We availed ourselves of the Fae departments at the British Museum. They have a superb collection of 16th century documents."

"Those guys at the museum never throw anything away," Lucas said amiably. "Some of the notebooks from the period are highly illuminating. Guess what we found out?"

"At this point," I said, "nothing is going to surprise me. What did you find out?"

"That Adeline Shevington had been secretly elected Ruling Elder over Reynold Isherwood three days before she was killed," Lucas replied. "The decision was to be announced the day *after* her death. Isherwood got the job by default."

"Adeline," I said to the woman in my mind, *"you've been holding out on me."*

Still sitting by the fire with Mr. Whiskers in her lap, she replied complacently, *"No dear, Reynold has been holding out on the entire Fae world. Listen."*

"There's more," Greer said. "Isherwood bribed the Creavit into good behavior with promises of positions within the Fae government and via arranged marriages with powerful magical families. He insisted, however, on the banishment of the *nonconformi* to the Middle Realm under the titular control of Fer Dorich. A solution Adeline adamantly campaigned against. Had she lived the Agreement would never have been put into place."

"But why was he so dead set on segregating half the Fae world?" I asked.

Festus cleared his throat. "Let me take that one."

Looking up at the sylph, the werecat said, "Excuse me, Sylvia? You mind floating down here for a second?"

The sylph shrank down to his level. "Yes, Master Cat?"

Festus chuckled, "'Master Cat,' I like that. Okay, so, did you know about the crystal necklace Sam kept locked in a chest in the attic?"

"I did. Sam said it must be guarded at all costs from The Thirty-Seven."

Tori voiced the group's confusion over that remark perfectly. "Oh freaking *great!* Thirty-seven what?"

Festus held up his paw. "Not so fast. Remember, Sam had dementia. I think he meant the necklace had to be guarded from the man who tried to take it in *1937*, a guy who could only want the crystal for one reason. To finish what he'd started. Kill Adeline Shevington once and for all."

And there it was. After all this time. The real reason Irenaeus Chesterfield was in Briar Hollow in 1937. He'd been looking for the crystal pendant holding Adeline's living essence.

At some point during the conversation, Rube had come out from under the desk and was now lounging on one of the leather sofas hanging on every word. Raccoons are serious conspiracy theory junkies.

"So," he said, his black eyes bright with excitement, "that means Chesterfield and Isherwood are in cahoots, right?"

I caught Adeline's eye in my thoughts. *"Are they?"*

"That is what we are going to London to find out."

AFTER WE ASSURED Sylvia we would not force her to return to the Middle Realm, we enjoyed a remarkably normal evening in the lair. Darby was over at the Pike House but left a buffet dinner in warming trays.

Glory dragged Greer off to one side to seek fashion advice

on acquiring a new, full-sized wardrobe and possibly changing her hairstyle. The poker game resumed once Marty and Leon came out of hiding, while Chase and Beau settled down for a game of chess.

Mom went home to spend the evening with Dad, while Tori and Gemma immersed themselves in alchemical experiments at their worktables. Lucas, suffering the effects of portal lag, stretched out on one of the sofas for a nap with his hat over his face.

Sylvia hovered happily from one group to the next, learning everyone's names and enjoying her newfound corporeality courtesy of the fairy mound. Duke was leary of her at first, but by the end of the evening, the ghost hound was following the sylph around with an adoring expression in his pale eyes.

Only Brenna was conspicuously absent, retreating to her room right after dinner. I was writing in my grimoire in the alcove when Adeline asked if she could take charge of my body for a few minutes.

"You want to talk to Brenna, don't you?"

"I do. I would like to alleviate some degree of her suffering if I can."

I gave Adeline permission to take over, happily settling into the privacy of my mind. Having another person sharing space in my head had an unexpected benefit; the rare ability for me to truly explore my inner space.

WHEN A KNOCK SOUNDED at the door of her bedroom, Brenna grimaced. She was in no mood to talk to anyone. "Come in," she said reluctantly, her face softening when she saw Jinx at the door.

"Jinx, I'm glad it's you . . . "

"Brenna, it's Adeline."

The sorceress paled, but still confronted her visitor with clear eyes. "Join me, please," she said, moving to vacate her chair.

"Don't get up. I can sit comfortably on the edge of the bed."

The two women faced one another over the short distance separating them. "I'm sure you have much that you wish to say to me," Brenna began stiffly. "All of which I most richly deserve."

"Cousin, I came to tell you that I bear you no malice for the night of my death."

Blinking as if she had not heard correctly, Brenna said, "That cannot be. Surely you know that in my Creavit state it could just as easily have been my hand that laid you low that night."

"We Sinclairs have many faults, but we have never been particularly given to murdering one another. At least no more than any other Scottish family."

In spite of herself, Brenna laughed, "Especially no more than any other *Highland* family."

"Indeed. You still believe your deal to become Creavit to be the shame of our clan. The shame lies in the actions of your father and brothers. Though they were Templars, they showed precious little nobility in your treatment. The defect of birth from which you suffered was not your fault."

"I seek now to live a different life," Brenna said earnestly. "I seek to be worthy of the name Sinclair."

"You have never lacked that worthiness. Your misdirection now plays to our advantage. I have need of your help in London. Will you stand by my side in bringing down Reynold Isherwood and Irenaeus Chesterfield?"

"My first loyalty," Brenna said, "is to the Witch of the Oak. So long as she fights by your side, so do I."

"Had your true destiny been fulfilled, *you* would be the Witch of the Oak."

"That fact is something I would prefer remain between us."

"The day will come when the entire story will be revealed. You cannot avoid that forever, cousin."

"Perhaps not forever," Brenna said, "but I can avoid it for now."

Chapter Twenty-Eight

With the revelation of Sylvia's identity, we effectively solved Cezar Ionescu's problem. Under Tori and Gemma's guidance, the hoodoo supplies were immediately removed and brought back to the lair to be cataloged.

You want to accomplish a speed move? Hire a crew of vampires.

As the crates started coming down the stairs, Glory was in her element, directing the stacking of the boxes in neat rows. Beau pried the lid off the first container, and they began to assign item numbers to the individual pieces. Thanks to the fairy mound, Glory now had a desk of her own and a full-sized computer with an enormous screen displaying the archive's database.

More of Sam's notebooks emerged as well, which Beau carefully set aside for immediate examination. Hopefully, the pages would contain confirmation that Chesterfield had been after the crystal pendant in 1937.

During one of Glory's excursions into the stacks, I went along so we could have a private talk. "Glory," I said, watching as she carefully shelved a box of graveyard dirt labeled by cemetery and plot holder, "I want you to know that if you want to return to your old life now, we'd all understand."

If I hadn't been quick on my feet, we'd have faced a major sweeping job.

"You're throwing me out?" she gasped, tears filling her eyes. "Aren't I doing a good enough job?"

"No . . . I mean, yes, you're doing a good job and no I'm not throwing you out," I stammered. "I'm saying that if you want to go back to the way you lived before Chesterfield cursed you, no one here will stop you."

Aligning the edge of the box perfectly with the lip of the shelf, Glory said, "I don't have a life to go back to, Jinx. You know, I searched the newspapers in Raleigh after I came here. By then I'd been missing for more than a year. There wasn't one story about me being gone, not one. So I checked the police department. Nobody filed a missing person's report. And at the archive? My old boss didn't look for me, he *fired* me for failing to show up to work!"

"What a jerk."

"You have no idea," Glory said, bobbing her head in agreement. "My whole life now is here working with all of you. I mean it. My whole, entire, *life*. Please don't make me go back to being ordinary again. I don't think I could stand it."

On impulse, I pulled her into a hug. "I don't think you were ever ordinary, Glory. You don't have to go anywhere, except back to your desk to finish cataloging all this hoodoo stuff."

She let out a happy squeal, embracing me with such bone shattering enthusiasm I could barely breathe. Then, as she stood back, she said shyly, "While it's just us, can I ask you a question?"

"Sure. What is it?"

"Would you be upset with me if I was sort of, kind of, maybe interested in Chase?"

You may think it would have been hard for me to get my head wrapped around the notion of effusive, adorably ditzy Glory with responsible, occasionally stodgy Chase, but you'd be wrong. The instant she said it, I not only saw how a relationship like that could work, I saw how it might be the best thing in the world for both of them.

"Don't be silly. Of course I'm not upset. Chase would be lucky to have someone like you. Go for it, with my blessings."

"Really? Oh my goodness, you are just the sweetest friend ever, ever, *ever!* Now, I've been thinking about maybe baking Chase a pie to get to know him better. Darby said I could use his kitchen, but I don't know what flavor to make . . . "

It would be several minutes before I managed to get a word in edgewise to tell her to go with buttermilk. In the interim, I enjoyed listening to her infectious enthusiasm. At my most smitten, I never gushed over Chase like that and seriously? He's the kind of guy who deserves to be gushed over.

We returned to the lair to find Festus and the raccoons teaching Sylvia how to play poker. I started to object until I heard her happy, lilting laughter. Air elemental or not, she'd been alone for a long time. Provided Festus didn't teach her to cheat, she deserved to have some fun.

After consulting with Adeline, Lucas and Greer had quietly returned to the British Museum the previous evening. She asked them to copy the relevant pages from the notebooks they'd already examined and to search for materials from other prominent Fae who might have taken notes during the Reformation.

When I kissed Lucas good-bye, I said, "Now remember, we have to go to Shevington in the morning to talk to Grandad and tomorrow night is Darby's party. The new *Haunted Briar Hollow* video will be live on YouTube, and he wants us all to see it."

"Will there be food?"

"You!" I said, punching his arm. "Always thinking with your stomach. It's Darby. Of course there'll be food, probably mountains of it."

"Don't worry. This is going to be a quick trip. In and out. The less attention we attract, the better. Oh, and we have to go by Harrods so Greer can get some things for Glory."

I fell asleep in my alcove that night and woke up to a beehive of activity. Darby, who was decorating for his party, had enlisted Sylvia's help to festoon the rafters with crepe paper. Beau and Glory were still hard at work, pressing the raccoons into service shelving items.

After a quick breakfast, Lucas, Greer, Festus, and I took off for our meeting in Shevington. We had to tell Barnaby and Moira about the link between Chesterfield and Isherwood, but none of us looked forward to the conversation.

As expected, Grandad erupted. He wanted to hop the first portal to London and confront the Ruling Elder immediately.

Moira and Adeline stopped him. I'd like to tell you what they talked about, but I can't because Adeline asked me to give them some privacy. They were in the study for more than two hours, during which time Festus insisted on dragging Lucas and Greer to the Dirty Claw for Litter Box Lager and darts.

When I caught up with them three hours later, it was in the wake of a private conversation between Barnaby and his late wife. When Adeline retreated in my consciousness, I stepped out of the study with Barnaby expecting Moira to be waiting for us. Instead, the front parlor stood empty.

Grandad looked at me with a stricken expression.

"Have you talked to her?" I asked.

He shook his head. "I don't know what to say."

The lameness of that statement made me want to slap the man.

"Well, I suggest you figure it out," I replied sharply. "She loves you, and this situation has to be hurting her."

I left him standing there looking dumbfounded, but I hoped with the motivation to get busy doing the right thing.

At the Dirty Claw, Lucas could tell I was troubled. "What is it?" he asked, leaning toward me so I could hear him over the roar of the werecats lining up to play darts with Greer. The baobhan sith was defeating all comers, but that didn't stop the shifters from taking her on anyway.

"Grandad hasn't talked to Moira about Adeline," I said. "I lost patience with him and told him to get himself down to her workshop and communicate with the poor woman. Now I feel bad that I barked at him."

"He's been through worse," Lucas said, signaling Manfred, the lynx bartender to bring us another round. "It sounds like he needed a push, so you gave him one."

"I know. I hope I pushed him in the right direction."

When we got back to Briar Hollow, I went upstairs to find the store deserted. Tori was alone in the espresso bar methodically cleaning the coffee machines.

"Where is everybody?" I asked, rolling up my sleeves and preparing to help her.

Disassembling a grinder, she said, "Everyone is in 'lull before the storm' mode — determined to get in one normal day before the next round of stuff hits the fan."

I groaned. "Tell me about it. We have to leave in a week. I convinced Barnaby I don't want to be in Shevington all the time, but he insisted we double up on the mirror call prep schedule starting tomorrow."

"How did he react to Festus' theory about Chesterfield and Isherwood?"

"Like you'd expect from a guy. He wanted to go to London and kick Isherwood's butt."

"I assume you stopped him."

"Moira and Adeline did, and then Adeline wanted to talk to him alone."

Tori stopped what she was doing. "How did Moira handle that?"

"She left while they were talking."

"Oh. I don't like the sound of that."

"Me either."

MOIRA SENSED Barnaby's approach long before he knocked at the door of her workshop. Suspecting he would come to her at some point, she had sent Dewey away earlier in the evening.

For once, the recalcitrant dwarf didn't argue. Instead, he'd paused on his way out and said gruffly, "You're the one he loves."

The sentiment, from such an unexpected source, brought tears to the alchemist's eyes. "He loved her first."

"You don't stop loving someone just because they died. Point is, you're here, in your own body. She's not."

With that, he turned on his heel and marched out leaving Moira to stare at the fire as she waited.

When Barnaby knocked, Moira didn't bother to go to the door. Instead she raised her hand and said, *"Fateri se."*

The alchemist listened as the hinges opened with a soft groan and closed again. Muffled footsteps crossed the flag-stones. When Moira still did not look away from the flames, Barnaby sat down in the chair next to her.

"Are you angry?" he asked quietly.

She sighed. "Angry that the essence of a woman who is like a sister to me lives? That we finally understand the reason for her murder and your brother's complicity in the deed? I would be a fool to be angry over such vital information."

"Then let me be more precise. Are you angry with me?"

Moira shook her head. "No, Barnaby, I'm not angry with you. I'm annoyed with myself. We are about to embark on a diplomatic mission that could alter the relationship of the realms forever, and I am allowing confusion to cloud my mind."

Shifting uneasily in his chair, Barnaby said, "I learned much this day that I did not know. That Adeline was to be the Ruling Elder, that she opposed the plan of segregation, that Reynold is most likely a traitor, and that I am an utter fool."

"Hardly, politics swirled at a rapid pace in those days."

"That's not what I'm talking about," he said, catching hold of her hand. "Please look at me."

When their eyes met, he said, "I love you, Moira. I have loved you lo these many years, but I have not been fair to you. I have not shouted our love from the rooftops but instead asked you to play out this ridiculous charade of secrecy. I apologize for that, my darling, and if you will allow me, I would like to ask you something."

"What?"

Still holding her hand, he dropped to one knee on the floor in front of her, "Will you marry me?"

From the shadows near the door, Dewey watched as the alchemist leaned forward and kissed the Lord High Mayor.

"About time," the dwarf said gruffly, coming into the room with a bottle of champagne and two glasses. "This was in the kitchen. Drink it before it goes bad. Congratulations."

He stomped out to the sound of their laughter making sure his back was turned so they couldn't see him smile.

Chapter Twenty-Nine

D arby transformed the lair into a festive space for the airing of *Haunted Briar Hollow: The Tacogeist*, but the fairy mound — in a show of support — outdid itself. We settled into two rows of plush, reclining theater seats with enormous bags of buttered popcorn to watch the show on the big screen TV. On cue, the lights dimmed, and a theatrical overture boomed around us.

The video opened with a familiar scene: the HBH kids gathered around the coffee table at the Pike house enjoying the tacos Tori sent over. At the point when Darby, in invisible mode, levitated the taco, a dark filter fell over the screen with a bright vignette highlighting the floating food.

"We were working at home when it happened," Nick's voice narrated, "the first appearance of the friendly spirit we've come to know as The Tacogeist. Immediately responsive to our attempts at communication, the entity repeatedly levitated objects in the room."

A moving collage splashed across the screen filled with twirling straws, bouncing napkins, and finally the spinning Rubix cube. "Encouraged that we were dealing with an intelligent haunting," Nick continued, "we began to put in place the infrastructure for a comprehensive investigation."

I glanced over at Darby. He was sitting in one of the massive chairs with his short legs sticking straight out staring up at the screen with a rapt expression — oblivious to Rube stealing popcorn on his right and Festus doing the same thing on his left.

"Imagine our shock," Nick said, "when we came down the next morning to discover the ghost had rearranged multiple objects in our house in what we can only describe as an act of housekeeping."

The camera panned over a now immaculate living room before passing into an equally sparkling kitchen. "It seems the ghost thinks we're slobs," Nick admitted, "but we think it's amazing."

Darby blushed with pleasure at the praise.

We were treated to in-depth explanations of the equipment the kids used, the placement of their infrared cameras, and speculation about the significance of the Pike House. "The former occupant, a reclusive elderly man named Fish Pike was killed at an undisclosed location," Nick said, "but his body was left in plain sight on the town square. Could the Tacogeist be Fish Pike himself? We asked local Sheriff John Johnson."

The lawman's face filled the screen. "You know I don't believe in this stuff," he said, clearly speaking to whoever was holding the camera, "but no, I don't think Fish would come back from the grave to clean house for you kids. I was in his place after he died and it wasn't up for the cover of *Good Housekeeping*."

Nick's narration resumed. "With no clue to the identity of the spirit, we resolved to try a variety of means to get the entity to converse with us."

That led to a squawky, discordant session with something called a spirit box before the ghost hunters settled down to do an EVP session, explaining to the viewers that electronic voice phenomenon tries to record ectoplasmic speech.

I saw Darby scoot closer toward the front of his seat until his feet dangled over the edge.

"We never in our wildest dreams anticipated this," Nick said. "We will now play for you what may be the most impressive EVP ever captured. During our session, we asked the Tacogeist multiple questions with no responses until Mindy did this."

The image went to the tell-tale reverse black and white of infrared imaging. Mindy, Kyle, and Nick were once again sitting around the coffee table. "Hi," Mindy said, speaking to the room in general. "If you can't tell us your name, can you tell us anything about life on the other side?"

After several seconds, Mindy said, "Oh my God! Did you guys hear that? Play back the tape, Kyle."

Her associate fumbled with the recorder.

"Turn up the volume!" she ordered. "Listen!"

Out of the machine's tiny speaker, Darby, in a thoroughly credible imitation of Elvis said,

"Thank you, thank you very much."

Glory squealed as she and the brownie exchanged an exuberant high five.

"And there you have it, folks," Nick said, "Elvis may not have left the building after all!"

As the closing credits played, the lights in the lair came up. Everyone crowded around Darby, congratulating him on his haunting skills. I was the only one who seemed to notice that the HBH kids did a postscript for their broadcast.

I couldn't make out what Nick was saying over the noise, so I stepped into the alcove and pulled out my iPhone. When I found the video on YouTube, I scrolled to the end and listened as Nick said, "Thank you for joining us for the latest installment of Haunted Briar Hollow. If you like what we're doing, please follow us on Twitter and like us on Facebook. On our next episode, we'll be looking at a report brought to us by local Jim Ed Elroy who observed a van rollover on a deserted highway caused by a mysterious white doe. Here's a sample of what Jim Ed told us."

The camera cut to a guy in a gimme cap who said earnestly, "It was the damnedest thing I've ever seen. This white deer just stood in the middle of the road and watched that van flip over two or three times and never moved — and when I looked back, that deer had disappeared. I'm telling you man, that deer was like a freaking ghost or something. Then I went to help those ladies, and I could have sworn I saw two coffins in the weeds."

Oh. Crap.

SERAPHINA RAN her hands along the edge of the desk. The director of the blood bank had tacky, pedestrian tastes, but matters of interior decoration could be handled. The woman had proven remarkably susceptible to glamour, as had the board of directors.

Once under her control, the weaklings were delighted to accept Seraphina as an expert in hematology, seeing credentials and licenses on the blank pieces of paper she slid before them. They turned control of the operation over to her without a whimper of protest, nodding in agreement when Seraphina fired the existing lab director in favor of Ioana.

The facility would continue to funnel enough blood to required outlets to keep their cover intact, but the Strigoi were now in possession of an almost limitless supply of protein. If the appointments were handled correctly, they could even indulge in the occasional warm snack with no one the wiser.

The ruse would only be necessary until they'd located the wizard, Chesterfield.

Seraphina leaned back in her desk chair and watched the video feed from the lobby. So many willing donors from which to pick. The front door opened, and a moderately built man came inside. Something about him seemed familiar.

Using the computer mouse, the Strigoi zoomed in as a slow grin spread over her face.

Scrap Andrews.

Sometimes the Fates were so very kind to good little vampires.

A Word from Juliette

Thank you for reading *To Haunt a Witch*. Now that you've reached the end of the book, I hope you'll want to continue the adventure with Jinx, Tori, and the gang in Briar Hollow and beyond.

The story develops through a page-turning series of urban fantasy novels that take the characters into new adventures and realms.

In the next story, To Test a Witch, readers are transported to Fae Londinium and the Conference of the Realms where an assassination attempt puts Barnaby's life in danger and leaves Jinx in charge of the Shevington delegation.

Not certain you want to continue the journey? I've included the first chapter of To Test a Witch to give you a sneak peak of the mystery, adventure, and hijinks lying ahead!

But first . . . Get Exclusive Jinx Hamilton Material

There are many things I love about being an author, but building a relationship with my readers is far and away the best.

Once a month I send out a newsletter with information on new releases, sneak peeks, and inside articles on Jinx Hamilton as well as other books and series I'm currently developing.

You can get all this and more by signing up here.

To Test a Witch -
Preview

Colonel Beau Longworth propped the heels of his boots against the plank seat in front of him and surveyed the new baseball field with satisfaction. Below the stands, on the well-manicured grass, the ghostly members of the Briar Hollow Spectral Sports League glowed dimly under the full moon.

"The Ionescus have quite outdone themselves in this expression of generosity toward the community," the colonel said, turning toward Chase and Glory who sat beside him sharing a bag of peanuts. "The local Little League teams will compete in spectacular style this spring."

Taking a drink of his soda, Chase said, "Cezar thought the town needed some cheering up after the Freak Freeze. According to Tori, the customers in the Witch's Brew are still talking about their disaster preparation plans for next winter."

"It is unfortunate that we cannot ease their fears with a true account of the incident, but I suspect that would only elevate their apprehensions to new and even more uncomfortable levels."

Glory ran her straw up and down in her cup to loosen the

ice. "Well, I think Mr. Ionescu had the right idea about donating this field to make everyone feel better. You know, the Witch's Brew is sponsoring one of the Little League teams. That's why Darby isn't here tonight. He's back in the lair working on the uniforms, and Tori is going to coach the kids."

Chase laughed. "Something tells me they'll learn more from her than baseball. Where is she?"

"Miss Tori departed for Shevington after Jinx and the others left for London," Beau said. "She felt the need to lend moral support to Connor in his new found position of authority. Barnaby has only been gone a few hours, and already the mantle of mayor pro tem does not rest easily on Connor's shoulders."

"I don't imagine it does," Chase said. "I sure wouldn't want that job."

"Nor would I," Beau agreed. "Having commanded men in the past, I wish for no authority beyond leading our league to victory this season. I have been anticipating spring training with great avidity, but I did not expect to be gifted with such a superb facility so near the cemetery. This is a most convenient arrangement."

"Convenient and *secure*," Chase said. "Cezar made sure the area is ringed with motion sensors 100 yards out. We're not going to have anymore screw ups like that viral video the Haunted Briar Hollow kids shot. If anyone approaches the field during one of the spectral games, the players will have more than enough time to *obscurate*."

Glory frowned. "Is that a baseball thing?" she asked, squeaking her straw against the plastic cup lid.

Chase laughed. "No. *Obscurate* means to dissipate from sight."

"Oh. You mean going invisible like Darby does."

"Not exactly," Beau explained. "The longer a being exists in the spectral plane, the more deft it becomes at modulating the degree of energy required to become visible or to interact with the human world. Cezar's warning system will allow our players the opportunity to . . . ."

He seemed to be struggling to find the right phrase.

"Dial it down?" Glory suggested helpfully.

"Yes!" Beau beamed. "That is the phrase for which I was searching. Miss Tori is of the opinion I should be less formal in my speech patterns. I have been trying to become skillful with 21st-century idioms, but I find some of the phrasings to be quite unfathomable."

"Join the club," Chase said. "I still want to use slang from the '30s and '40s, but if you tell someone they're the 'bee's knees' these days, they'll think you've lost your mind."

"Oh, *I* wouldn't!" Glory said. "I love those decades. Everyone was glamorous, and the war was *so* romantic. Well, I mean Hollywood made it *seem* romantic, which it wasn't — outside of the movies. All those innocent people getting shot and bombed was horrible and tragic, but you know what I mean, about the romantic part, right?"

Smiling at her fondly, Chase said, "I know what you mean. Remind me to show you a picture of myself in the Forties. I still miss trousers with pleats."

Glory's face lit up. "Would you really show me the picture? It's so fascinating that you're 87 and you look so young and hand . . ."

Her voice trailed off as a red blush spread over her cheeks.

Chase came to her rescue with a simple "thank you" before adding jauntily, "I think I'm holding up pretty well if I do say so myself."

"*Oh,* " Glory said, bobbing her head up and down. "You are. You really are."

That vaulted both of them into sudden embarrassment. Studiously diverting their eyes back toward the field, they focused on watching Duke, Beau's ghostly coonhound, "helping" with batting practice by chasing down the balls and returning them to the basket that sat on the mound beside the team's pitcher, Hiram Folger.

"Hiram's looking good this spring," Chase said, steering the conversation firmly back to baseball.

"We are most fortunate that he died while his arm was still strong," Beau said, apparently oblivious to how cold the observation sounded. "I have been researching the death dates for a number of the deceased professionals among our opponents. Happily, many of them were quite long of tooth at their demise and no doubt beset with arthritis."

"*Beau!*" Glory said, in a scandalized tone. "You sound like you're happy those people got old and sick!"

The colonel looked at her beatifically, but with a spark of amusement in his eyes. "Would you not be equally outraged were I to exult that some of them died young and healthy, a fate typically regarded as a tragedy?"

Glory's mouth settled into a firmly disapproving line. "Oh! *You!*" she scolded. "Tori is right! You have to stop using all those pretty words! I can't ever decide if I'm supposed to be mad at you or not when you're talking circles around me."

"A skill most men would find quite useful when dealing with a woman," Beau replied gravely.

At that, Chase burst out laughing, and after thinking about it for a second, Glory joined in. Beau chuckled and said, "I believe this is an instance when it would be appropriate to say 'got you.'"

"Almost," Glory said, "but it's 'gotcha.' Try again."

Beau tried and failed completely, touching off another round of laughter. Wiping his eyes, he said, "I feel rather guilty that we are out here enjoying ourselves when matters of such great import are set to transpire in London."

"Don't be," Chase said, shelling another peanut. "All that political stuff will catch up with us soon enough. I, for one, am perfectly happy we're sitting where we are and that nothing sinister is going on in our world."

"Oh, Chase!" Glory gasped. "Don't *ever* say something like that! You're asking for trouble!"

"That's silly superstition," he scoffed. "The eyes of the whole Fae world are on London. Nobody's paying any attention to Briar Hollow. Enjoy the lull while it lasts."

No sooner were the words out of his mouth than a faintly glowing baseball careened into the stands, striking his cup, and drenching them all in a sticky rain of soda.

From the field, Hiram called, "Sorry, folks! Reckon I'm too juiced up tonight."

Glory looked at Chase with a wide-eyed "I told you so" expression made all the more incongruous by the single drop of soda hanging suspended at the end of her nose.

"See what you've done?" she said. "It's started already."

Scrubbing at his face with his hand, Chase said, "What's started already?"

"I don't know," she insisted, "but something definitely has, which is what you get for tempting fate."

Chase reached out and wiped away the soda drop. "You're cute when you get mad."

"Oh!" she fumed. "Don't *you* start talking pretty now! I'm telling you something awful is coming . . . did you call me cute?"

"Uh huh. I did. You want to go to a dance with me tomorrow night?"

For a second, the question rendered the voluble woman speechless. Then she nodded. "I'd like that, but I still say something bad is gonna happen."

"You're absolutely right," Chase answered somberly. "There's a very good chance I will step on your feet."

Also by Juliette Harper

In the Jinx Hamilton Series:

ALL Books Available in KindleUnlimited!

To Test a Witch

Book 9 transports readers to Fae Londinium. As the Conference of the Realms convenes, Jinx and the gang settle into adjoining rooms at Claridge's determined to find a way to end The Agreement segregating the In Between.

In the three days before the opening ceremony, Lucas assumes the role of tour guide, taking Jinx to Hampton Court and the British Museum. But it's the sites he doesn't show her that prove to be the most critical after an assassination attempt puts Barnaby's life in danger and leaves Jinx in charge of the Shevington delegation.

From encountering the ghosts of Henry VIII's wives to meeting a troop of gargoyle guards in the Fae Houses of Parliament, Jinx and her friends take the town by storm.

Buy To Test a Witch

In the Jinx Hamilton/ Wrecking Crew Novellas:

Moonstone

Werecat Festus McGregor leads his Recovery of Magical Objects Squad on a mission to retrieve the Moonstone Spoon from the penthouse of eccentric financier and collector Wardlaw Magwilde. Festus has the operation planned to the last detail until a wereparrot and a member of his own team throw a monkey wrench in the works -- but thankfully no actual monkeys.

Join Festus, Rube and the rest of the raccoons in this fun-filled novella from the bestselling author of the Jinx Hamilton series. Filled with hysterical Fae acronyms and overlapping agency jurisdictions, Moonstone is an escapist romp you won't want to put down.

Buy Moonstone

Merstone

A werecat and a raccoon walk into a dragon's lair . . .

Join ROMO agent and werecat Festus McGregor in this second installment of the Jinx Hamilton/ Wrecking Crew novellas. Agreeing to an off-the-books mission with wereparrot Jilly Pepperdine, Festus and Rube find themselves on the Isle of Wight in search of an ancient lodestone with the power to enslave shifters.

The perfect match of whimsical fun and fantastical adventure, enjoy the latest novella from bestselling author Juliette Harper. An escapist romp in the Fae world where magic, artifacts, and laughter abound!

Buy Merstone

The Selby Jensen Paranormal Mysteries

Descendants of the Rose

Selby Jensen's business card reads "Private Investigator," but that seriously downplays her occupation. Let's hear it in her own words:

"You want to know what I do for a living? I rip souls out. Cut heads off. Put silver bullets where silver bullets need putting. You think there aren't any monsters? . . . I have some disturbing news for you. You might want to sit down. Monsters walk among us. I'm looking for one in particular. In the meantime? I'm keeping the rest of them from eating people like you."

Juliette Harper, author of The Jinx Hamilton Novels, creates a cast of characters, most of whom have one thing in common; they don't have a pulse. The dead are doing just fine by Selby, who is determined never to lose someone she loves again, but then a force of love more powerful than her grief changes that plan.

Join Selby Jensen as she and her team track down a shadowy figure tied to a murder at a girls' school. What none of them realize, however, is that in solving this case, they will enter a longer battle against a larger evil.

Buy Descendants of the Rose

The Study Club Mysteries

You Can't Get Blood Out of Shag Carpet

Wanda Jean Milton discovers her husband, local exterminator Hilton Milton, dead on her new shag carpet with an Old Hickory carving knife sticking out of his chest.

Beside herself over how she'll remove the stain, and grief-stricken over Hilton's demise, Wanda Jean finds herself the prime suspect. But she is also a member of "the" local Study Club, a bastion of independent Texas feminism 1960s style.

Club President Clara Wyler has no intention of allowing a member to be a murder suspect. Aided by her younger sister and County Clerk, Mae Ella Gormley; Sugar Watson, the proprietress of Sugar's Style and Spray; and Wilma Schneider, Army MASH veteran and local RN, the Club women set out to clear Wanda Jean's name — never guessing the local dirt they'll uncover.

Buy You Can't Get Blood Out of Shag Carpet

About the Author

"It's kind of fun to do the impossible." Walt Disney said that, and the two halves of Juliette Harper believe it wholeheartedly. Together, Massachusetts-based Patricia Pauletti, and Texan Rana K. Williamson combine their writing talents as Juliette. "She" loves to create strong female characters and place them in interesting, challenging, painful, and often comical situations. Refusing to be bound by genre, Juliette's primary interest lies in telling good stories. Patti, who fell in love with writing when she won her first 8th grade poetry contest, has a background in music, with a love of art and design. Rana, a former journalist and university history instructor, is happiest with a camera in hand and a cat or two at home.

For more information . . .
www.JulietteHarper.com
admin@julietteharper.com

By Juliette Harper
Copyright 2017, Juliette Harper

Skye House Publishing, LLC

License Notes

eBooks are not transferable. All rights are reserved. No part of this book may be used or reproduced in any manner without written permission, except in the case of brief quotations embodied in critical articles and reviews. The unauthorized reproduction or distribution of this copyrighted work is illegal. No part of this book may be scanned, uploaded, or distributed via the Internet or any other means, electronic or print, without the author's permission.

This is a work of fiction. Names, characters, businesses, places, events, and incidents are either the products of the author's imagination or used in a fictitious manner. Any resemblance to actual persons, living or dead, or actual events is purely coincidental.

EBOOK ISBN: 978-1-943516-51-3

PRINT ISBN: 978-1-943516-52-0

Created with Vellum

Made in the USA
Monee, IL
16 October 2020

45332909R00142